Selected Stories

Poetry by Iain Crichton Smith
from Carcanet

The Exiles
Selected Poems
A Life
The Village and other poems

Iain Crichton Smith

SELECTED STORIES

CARCANET

This selection first published in Great Britain 1990 by
Carcanet Press Limited
208–212 Corn Exchange Buildings
Manchester M4 3BQ

Most of these stories have been taken from previous collections: *Survival without Error, The Village, The Black and the Red, Murdo and Other Stories*, and *Mr Trill and Other Stories*. Others have appeared in *Aberdeen University Review, Encounter, Radical Scotland, The Scotsman, Scottish Short Stories, Stand, 2 Plus 2*. Some have been adapted for broadcasting.

British Library Cataloguing in Publication Data

Smith, Iain Crichton *1928-*
  Selected stories.
  I. Title
  823'. 914 [F]

  ISBN 0-85635-869-X

The publisher acknowledges financial assistance
from the Arts Council of Great Britain

Typeset in 11pt Bembo by Bryan Williamson, Darwen
Printed and bound in England by SRP Ltd, Exeter

Contents

The Telegram

THE two women – one fat and one thin – sat at the window of the thin woman's house, drinking tea and looking down the road which ran through the village. They were like two birds, one a fat domestic bird, perhaps, the other more aquiline, more gaunt, or to be more precise, more like a buzzard.

It was war-time and though the village appeared quiet, much had gone on there. Reverberations from a war fought far away had reached it: many of its young men had been killed, since nearly all of them joined the navy, and their ships had sunk in seas which they had never seen except on maps which hung on the walls of the local school which they had all at one time or another unwillingly attended. One had been drowned on a destroyer after a leave during which he had told his family that he would never come back again (or at least that was the rumour in the village which was still, as it had always been, a superstitious place). Another had been drowned during the pursuit of the *Bismarck*.

What the war had to do with them, the people of the village did not know. It came on them as an alien plague, taking their sons away and then killing them meaninglessly, randomly. They watched the road often for the telegrams.

The telegrams were brought to the houses by the local church elder who, clad in black, would walk along the road and then stop at the house to which the telegram was directed. People began to think of the telegram as a strange missile pointed at them from abroad. They did not know what to associate it with, certainly not with God, but it was a weapon of some kind, it picked a door and entered, and left desolation just like any other weapon.

The two women who watched the street were different from each other, not only physically but socially. For the thin woman's son was a sub-lieutenant in the Navy, while the fat woman's son was only an ordinary seaman. The fat woman's son had to salute the thin woman's son. One got more pay than the other and wore a better uniform. One had been at university, the other had left school at the age of fourteen.

When they looked out of the window they could see cows wandering lazily about, but little other movement. The fat woman's cow used to eat the thin woman's washing, and the latter was looking out for it but she couldn't see it. The thin woman was not popular in the village. She was an incomer from another village and had only been in this one for thirty years or so. The fat woman had lived in the village all her days: she was a native. Also the thin woman was ambitious: she had sent her son to university though she had only a widow's pension of ten shillings a week.

As they watched they could see at the far end of the street the tall man in black clothes carrying in his hand a piece of yellow paper. This was a bare village with little colour and therefore the yellow was both strange and unnatural.

The fat woman said, 'It's the Macleod again.'

They were both frightened, for he could be coming to their house. And so they watched him, and as they did so they spoke feverishly as if by speaking continually and studying his every move they would be able to keep from themselves whatever plague he was bringing.

The thin woman said, 'Don't worry, Sarah, it won't be for you. Donald only left home last week.'

'You don't know,' said the fat woman, 'you don't know.' And then she added, without thinking, 'It's different for the officers.'

'Why is it different for the officers?' said the thin woman in an even voice without taking her eyes from the black figure.

'Well, I just thought they're better off,' said the fat woman confusedly, 'they get better food and better conditions.'

'They're still on the ship,' said the thin woman, who was thinking that the fat woman was very stupid. But then most of the villagers were: they were large, fat, and lazy. Most of them could have afforded better than her to send their sons and daughters to universities but they didn't want to be thought of as snobbish.

'They are that,' said the fat woman. 'But your son is educated,' she added irrelevantly. Of course her son didn't salute the thin woman's son if they were both at home on leave at the same time. It had happened once that they had been. But naturally there was an uneasiness and distance between them.

'I made sacrifices to have my son educated,' said the thin woman. 'I lived on a pension of ten shillings a week. I was in nobody's debt. More tea?'

'No, thank you,' said the fat woman. 'He's passed Bessie's house. That means it can't be Roddy. He's safe.'

For a terrible moment she realized that she had hoped that the elder would have turned in at Bessie's house. Not that she had anything against Bessie or Roddy. But still one thought of one's own family first.

The thin woman continued remorselessly as if she were pecking away at something she had pecked at for years. 'The teacher told me to send Iain to university. He came to see me. I had no thought of sending him before he came. "Send your son to university," he said to me. "He's got a good head on him." And I'll tell you, Sarah, I had to count every penny. Ten shillings isn't much. When did you see me with good clothes in the church?'

'That's true,' said the fat woman absently. 'We have to make sacrifices.' It was difficult to know what she was thinking of – the whale meat or the saccharins? Or the lack of clothes? Her mind was vague and diffused except when she was thinking about herself.

The thin woman continued, 'Many's the time I used to sit here in this room and knit clothes for him when he was young. I even knitted trousers for him. And for all I know he may marry an English girl, and where will I be then? He might go and work in England. He was staying in a house there at Christmas. He met a girl at a dance and he found out later that her father was the town mayor. I'm sure she smokes and drinks. And he might not give me anything after all I've done for him.'

'Donald spends all his money,' said the fat woman. 'He never sends me anything. When he comes home on leave he's never in the house, I hardly see him. But I don't mind. He was always like that. Meeting strangers and buying them drinks. It's his nature and he can't go against his nature. He's passed the Smiths. That means Tommy's all right.'

There were only three houses left before he would reach her own house, and then the last one was the one where she was sitting.

'I think I'll take a cup of tea right enough,' she said. And then, 'I'm sorry about that cow.' But no matter how you tried you could never like the thin woman. She was always putting on airs. Mayor indeed! Sending her son to university! Why did she want to be better than anyone else? Saving and scrimping all the time. And everybody said that her son wasn't as clever as all that: he had failed some of the university exams too. Her own son Donald was just as clever and could have gone to university, but he was too fond of fishing and being out with the boys.

As she drank her tea her heart was beating fast and she was frightened, and she didn't know what to talk about and yet she wanted to talk. She liked talking, after all what else was there to do? But the thin woman didn't gossip much. You couldn't feel at ease with her, you had the idea all the time that she was thinking about something else, something more important than gossip.

The thin woman came and sat down beside her.

'Did you hear,' said the fat woman, 'that Malcolm Mackay was on a drink-driving charge? He smashed his car, so they say. It was in the black-out.'

'I didn't hear that,' said the thin woman.

'It was when he was coming home last night with the butcher meat. He had it in the van and he smashed the car at the burn. But they say he's all right. I don't know how he managed to keep out of the war. They said something was wrong with his heart, but there was nothing wrong with it. What's wrong with his heart if he can drink and smash a car?'

The thin woman drank her tea very carefully. She had been away in service a long time before she had married and she had a dainty way of doing things. She sipped her tea, her little finger curled round the cup in an elegant, irritating way.

'Why do you keep your finger like that?' said the fat woman suddenly.

'Like what?'

The fat woman demonstrated.

'Oh, it was the way I saw the guests drinking tea in the hotels when I was in service. They always drank like that.'

'He's passed the Stewarts,' said the fat woman. Two houses to go. They looked at each other wildly. It must be one of them. Surely. They could see the elder quite clearly now, walking very stiff, very upright, wearing his hard black hat. He walked in a stately, dignified manner, his eyes staring straight ahead of him.

'He's proud of what he's doing,' said the fat woman suddenly. 'You'd think he was proud of it. Knowing the news before anyone else. And he himself was never in the war.'

'Yes,' said the thin woman. 'It gives him a position.' They watched him. He was a stiff, quiet man who kept himself to himself, more than ever now. He didn't mix with people, and it was him who carried the Bible into the pulpit for the minister.

'They say his wife had one of her fits again,' said the fat woman viciously. He had passed the Murrays. The next house was her own. She sat perfectly still. Oh pray God the message wasn't for her. And yet it must be for her. Surely it must be for her. She had dreamt of this happening, her son drowning in the Atlantic Ocean, her own child whom she had reared, whom she had seen going to play football in his green jersey and white shorts, whom she had seen running home from school. She could see him drowning, but she couldn't make out the name of the ship. She had never seen a really big ship and the picture she had in her mind was more like the mail-boat than a cruiser. Her son couldn't drown there for no reason that she could understand. God couldn't do that to people. God was kinder than that. God helped you in your sore trouble. She began to mutter a prayer over and over. She said it quickly like the Catholics, O God save my son, O God save my son, O God save my son. She was ashamed of prattling in that way, as if she was counting beads, but she couldn't stop herself, and on top of that she would soon cry. She knew it, and she didn't want to cry in front of the thin woman, that foreigner. It would be weakness. She felt the arm of the thin woman around her shoulders, the thin arm, and it was like first love, it was like that time Murdo had taken her hand in his when they were coming home from the dance, such an innocent gesture, such a spontaneous gesture. So unexpected, so strange, so much a gift. She was crying and she couldn't bring herself to look...

'He has passed your house,' said the thin woman in a distant, firm voice, and she looked up. He was walking along and he had indeed passed her house. She wanted to stand up and dance all round the kitchen, the poor kitchen, all fifteen stone of her, and shout and cry and sing a song, but then she stopped. She couldn't do that. How could she do that when it must be the thin woman's son? There was no other house. The thin woman was looking out at the elder, her lips pressed closely together, white and bloodless. Where had she learnt that self-control? She wasn't crying or shaking. She was looking out at something which she had always dreaded, but she wasn't going to cry or surrender or give herself away to anyone.

And at that moment the fat woman saw. She saw the years of discipline, she remembered how thin and unfed and pale the thin woman had always looked, how sometimes she had to borrow money, even a shilling, to buy food. She saw what it must have been like to be a widow bringing up a son in a village not her own. She saw it so clearly that she was astounded. It was as if she had an extra vision, as if the air itself brought the past with all its details nearer. The number of times the thin woman had been ill, and people said that she was weak and useless. She looked down at the thin woman's arm. It was so shrivelled and dry.

And the elder walked on. A few yards now till he reached the wooden plank which crossed the ditch in front of the thin woman's house. But the thin woman hadn't cried. She was steady and still, her lips still compressed, sitting upright in her chair. And, miracle of miracles, the elder passed the plank, and walked straight on.

They looked at each other. What did it all mean? Where was the elder going, clutching the telegram in his hand, walking like a man in a daze. There were no other houses, so where was the elder going? They drank their tea in silence, turning away from each other. The fat woman said, 'I must be going.' They parted without speaking. The thin woman still sat at the window, looking out. Once or twice the fat woman made as if to turn back, as if she had something to say, some message to pass on, but she didn't. She walked away.

It wasn't till later that night that they discovered what had happened. The elder had a telegram directed to himself, to tell him of the drowning of his own son. He should never have seen it just like that, but there had been a mistake at the post office, owing to the fact that there were two boys in the village with the same name. His walk through the village was a somnambulistic wandering. He didn't want to go home to tell his wife what had happened. He was walking along not knowing where he was going, when he was stopped half way to the next village. Perhaps he was going in search of his son. Altogether he had walked six miles. The telegram was crushed in his hand and so sweaty that they could hardly make out the writing.

Timoshenko

WHEN I went into the thatched house as I always did at nine o'clock at night, he was lying on the floor stabbed with a bread knife, his usually brick-red face pale and his ginger moustache a dark wedge under his nose. His eyes were wide open like blue marbles. I wondered where she was. The radio was still on and I went over and switched it off. At the moment she came down from the other room and sat on the bench. There was no point in going for a doctor; he was obviously dead: even I could tell that. She sat like a child, her knees close together, her hands folded in her lap.

I had regarded the two of them as children. He had a very bad limp and sat day after day at the earthen wall which bordered the road, his glassy hands resting on his stick, talking to the passers-by. Sometimes he would blow on his fingers, his cheeks red and globular. She on the other hand sat in the house most of the time, perhaps cooking a meal or washing clothes. Of the two I considered her the simpler, though she had been away from the island a few times, in her youth, at the fishing, but had to be looked after by the other girls in case she did something silly.

'Did you do that?' I said, pointing to the body which seemed more eloquent than either of us. She nodded wordlessly. As a matter of fact I hadn't liked him very much. He was always asking me riddles to which I did not know the answer, and when I was bewildered he would nod his head and say, 'I don't understand what they are teaching at these schools nowadays.' He had an absolutely bald head which shone in the light, and a sarcastic way of speaking. He would call his sister Timoshenko or Voroshilov, because the Russians at that time were driving the Germans out of their country and these generals were always in the news. 'Timoshenko will know about it,' he would say and she would stand there smiling, a teapot in her hands.

But of course I never thought what it was like for the two of them when I wasn't there. Perhaps he persecuted her. Perhaps his sarcasm was a perpetual wound. Perhaps, lame as he was, sitting at the wall all day, he was petrified by boredom and his tiny mind squirmed like the snail-like meat inside a whelk. He had never left the island in his whole life and I didn't know what had caused his limp which was so serious that he had to drag himself along by means of two sticks.

The blood had stopped flowing and the body lay on the floor like a log. The fire was out and the dishes on the dresser were clean and colourful rising in tier after tier. The floor which was made of clay seemed to undulate slightly. I felt unreal as if at any moment the body would rise from the floor like a question mark and ask me another riddle, the moustache twitching like an antenna. But this didn't happen. It stayed there solid and heavy, the knife sticking from its breast.

I knew that soon I would have to get someone, perhaps the policeman or a doctor or perhaps a neighbour. But I was so fascinated by the woman that I stayed, wondering why she had done it. Girlishly she sat on the bench, her hands in her lap, not even twisting them nervously.

Suddenly she said, 'I don't know why but I took the knife and I...I don't know why.'

She looked past me, then added, 'I can't remember why I did it. I don't understand.'

I waited for her to talk and after a while she went on.

'Many years ago,' she said, 'I was going to be married. He made fun of me when Norman came into the house. He said I couldn't cook and I couldn't wash, and that was wrong. That must have been twenty years ago. He was limping then too. He told Norman I was a bit daft. That was many years ago. But that wasn't it. Anyway, he told Norman I was silly. Norman had put on his best suit when he came to the house. He wasn't rich or anything like that. You didn't know him. Anyway he's dead now. He died last week in the next village. He was on his own and they found him in the house dead. He had been dead for a week; of course he was quite old. He was older than me then. Anyway he came into the house and he was wearing his best suit and he had polished his shoes and I thought that he looked very handsome. Well, Donald said that I wasn't any good at cooking and that I was silly. He made fun of me and all the time he made fun of me Norman looked at me, as if he wanted me to say something. I remember he had a white handkerchief in his pocket and it looked very clean. Norman didn't have much to say for himself. In those days he worked a croft, and he was building a house. I was thirty years old then and he was forty-two. I was wearing a long brown skirt which I had got at the fishing and I was sitting as I am sitting now with my hands in my lap as my mother taught me. Donald said that I smoked when I was away from home. That was wicked of him. Of course to him it was a joke but it wasn't true. I think Norman believed him and he didn't like women smoking. My brother, you see, would make jokes all the time, they were like knives in my body, and my mind wasn't quick enough to say something back to him. Norman maybe didn't love me but we would have been happy together. Donald believed that his jokes were very funny, that people looked up to him, and that he was a clever man. But of course he...Maybe if it hadn't been for his limp he might have carried on in school, so he said anyway. I left school at twelve. I had to look after him even when my parents were alive.

'It didn't matter what I did, it was wrong. The tea was too hot or too cold. The potatoes weren't cooked right or the herring wasn't salt enough. "Who would marry you?" he would say to me. But I think Norman would have married me. Norman was a big man but he was slow and honest. He wasn't sarcastic at all and he couldn't think like my brother.

"She was in Yarmouth," Donald told him, "but they won't have her back, she's too stupid. Aren't you, Mary?" he asked me. That wasn't true. The reason I couldn't go to Yarmouth was because I had to stay at home and look after him. I was going to go but he made me stop. He got very ill the night before I was due to leave and I had to stay behind. Anyway Norman went away that night and he never came back. I can still see him going out the door in his new suit back to the new house he was building. I found out afterwards that my brother had seen him and told him that I used to have fits at the time of the new moon, and that wasn't true.

'So I never married, and Donald would say to me, if I did something that he didn't like, "That's why Norman never married you, you're too stupid. And you shouldn't be going about with your stockings hanging down to your ankles. It doesn't look ladylike." '

I remembered how I used to come and listen to the News in this very house and it would tell of the German armies being inexorably strangled by the Russians. I would have visions of myself like Timoshenko standing up in my tank with dark goggles over my eyes as the Germans cowered in the snow and the rope of cold was drawn tighter and tighter. And he would say to me, 'Now then, tell me how many mackerel there are in a barrel. Go on now, tell me that.' And he would put his bald head on one side and look at me, his ginger moustache bristling. Or he would say, 'Tell me, then, what is the Gaelic for a compass. Eh? The proper Gaelic, I mean. Timoshenko will tell you that. Won't you, Timoshenko? She was at the fishing, weren't you, Timoshenko?'

And he would shift his aching legs, sighing heavily, his face becoming redder and redder.

'He thought I knew nothing,' she said. 'Other times he would threaten to put me out of the house because it belongs to him, you see.' She looked down at the body as if he were still alive and he were liable to stand up and throw her out of the house, crowing like a cockerel, his red cheeks inflated, and his red wings beating.

'He would say, "I'll get a housekeeper in. There's plenty who would make a good housekeeper. You're so stupid you don't know anything. And you leave everything so dirty. Look at this shirt you're supposed to have washed!"'

Was all this really true, I wondered. Had this woman lived in this village for so many years without anyone knowing anything about her suffering? It seemed so strange and unreal. All the time we had thought of the two as likeable comedians and one was cruel and vicious and the other was tormented and resentful. We had thought of them as nice, pleasant people, characters in the village. We didn't think of them as people at all, human beings who were locked in a death struggle. When people talked about her she became a sunny figure out of a comic, blundering about in a strange English world when she left the island, but happy all the same. We hadn't imagined that she was suffering like this in her dim world. And when we saw him sitting by the wall we thought of him as a fixture and we would shout greetings to him and he would shout back some quaint witticism. How odd it all was.

'But I knew what was going on all the time,' she continued. 'I could follow the news too. I knew what the Germans were doing, and the Russians. But he made me out to be a fool. And the thing was even after I heard of Norman's death I didn't say anything, though he said a few things himself. He told me one day, "You should have been his housekeeper and he wouldn't have been found dead like that on his own. But you weren't good enough for him. Poor man." And he would look at me with those small eyes of his. They had found Norman, you see, by the fire. He had fallen into it, he was ill and old. He hadn't been well for years. I often thought of taking him food but Donald wouldn't let me. After all we're all human and a little food wouldn't have been missed. I used to think of when we were young so many years ago. And when I was young I wasn't ugly. I wasn't beautiful but I wasn't ugly. I used to go to the dances when I was young, like the others. And of course I was at Yarmouth. He had never been out of the island though he was a man and I was only a woman and we used to bring presents home at the end of the season. I bought him a pipe once and another time I got him a melodeon but he wouldn't play it. So you see, there was that.'

There was another longish silence. Outside, it was pitch black and there was ice on the roads. In fact coming over from my own house I nearly slipped and fell but I had a torch so that was all right.

I wasn't at all afraid of her. I was in a strange way enjoying our conversation or rather her monologue. It was as if I was listening to an important story about life, a warning and a disaster. I remembered how as children we would be frightened by her brother waving his sticks from the wall where he was sitting. And we would run away full tilt as if we were running away from a monster. Our parents would say, 'It's only his joking,' and think how kind he was to go out of his way to entertain the children, but I wondered now whether in fact it might not be that he hated children and it wasn't acting at all, that cockerel clapping his sticks at us as we scattered across the moor.

Maybe too he had been more in pain than we had thought.

The trouble was that we didn't visit the two of them much at all. I did so, but only because I wished to listen to their radio to hear the news. Also, I was a quiet, reserved person who was happier in the company of people older than myself. But I hadn't actually looked at either of them with a clear hard look. To me she was a simple creature who smiled when her brother made some joke about Timoshenko, for his jokes tended to be remorselessly repetitive. It didn't occur to me that she was perhaps being pierced to the core by his primitive witticisms and it didn't occur to me either that they were meant to be cruel and were in fact outcrops from a perpetual war.

Suddenly she said to me, 'Would you like a cup of tea?' Without thinking I said 'Yes,' as if it was the most natural remark in the world while the body lay on the floor between us. I was amazed at how calmly I had accepted the presence of the body, though I had always thought of myself as sensitive and delicate. But on the other hand it was as if the body was not real, as if, as I have said, it would get to its feet, place its sticks under its arms, and walk towards me asking me riddles. Naturally however this didn't happen. And so we drank the tea out of neat cups with thin blue stripes at the rim.

'I had to give him all my saccharins,' she said, 'because he liked sweet things. It's a long time since I've had such a sweet cup of tea.' I noticed then that she had put saccharins in my tea and I realized that this was the first time that I had had tea in her house. She was in a strange way savouring her transient freedom.

'I remember now,' she said. 'It was the Germans and Timoshenko. The Germans had been trying to destroy Russia. I knew that, I'm not daft. And now the Russians were killing them. I heard that on the six o'clock news. And Timoshenko, he was doing that, he was winning. It was then that I . . .' She stopped then, the cup at her lips. 'I remember now. It was when it said about Timoshenko and he said the tea wasn't sweet enough. That was when I . . . I must have been cutting bread. I must . . .'

She looked at me in amazement as if it was just at that moment that she realized she had killed him. As she began to tremble I took the cup from her hands – it was spilling over – and put my arm around her and comforted her while she cried.

By their Fruits

MY Canadian uncle told me, 'Today we are going to see John Smith. I'll tell you a story about him. When he was nineteen years old, and coming to Canada, the minister met him and he said to him (you see, John had been working at the Glasgow shipyards before that) the minister said to him, "And I hear you've been working on a Sunday," and John said to him, "I hear you work on a Sunday yourself." So when John was leaving to come to Canada the minister wouldn't speak to him. Imagine that. He was nineteen years old, the minister didn't know whether he would ever see him again. Now the fact is that John has never been to church since he came to Canada.'

My uncle was eighty-six years old. He had been allowed to drive, I think, during the duration of our holiday with him, and he took full advantage of the concession.

'They said to me,' he told us, 'you keep out of Vancouver, you can drive around your home area, old timer. Drive around White Rock.'

Every morning he took the white Plymouth from the garage, put on his glasses carefully and set off with us for a drive of hundreds of miles, perhaps to Hell's Gate or Fraser River. His wife was dead: in the garden he had planted a velvety red rose in remembrance of her, and he watered it devoutly every day.

Once in Vancouver we came to a red light which we drove through, while a woman who was permitted to cross in her car stared at him, her mouth opening and shutting like that of a fish.

'These women drivers,' he said contemptuously, as he drove negligently onwards.

Every summer he took the plane home to Lewis. 'What I do,' he said, 'I leave this lamp on so that people think I am here.' One summer Donalda and I searched Loch Lomondside for the house in which his wife had been born but we couldn't find it.

'She was an orphan, you know, and the way we met was like this. She went to London on service and decided she would emigrate to Australia, but then changed her mind when she saw an advertisement showing British Columbia and its fruit. I was going to Australia myself with another fellow, but he dropped out so I emigrated to Canada instead. One night at a Scottish Evening in Vancouver I saw her coming in the door wearing a yellow dress. I knew at that moment that that was the girl for me, so I asked her for a dance, and that was how it happened.'

He fixed his eye on the road. 'Listen,' he said, 'you can drive a few miles over the limit. You're allowed to do that.' His big craggy face was tanned like a Red Indian's. It was like an image you would see on a totem pole.

John Smith lived in a house which was not as luxurious as my uncle's. He had a limp, and immediately my uncle came in he began to banter with him.

'Here he is,' he said to his wife, 'the Widows' Delight.' My uncle smiled.

'Listen,' he said to me, after he had introduced me. 'This fellow believes that we come from monkeys,' and he smiled again largely and slightly contemptuously.

'That's true enough,' said Smith, stretching his leg out on the sofa where he was sitting. His wife said nothing but watched the two of them. She was a large woman with a flat white face.

'It may be true of you,' said my uncle, 'but it's not true of me. I'm not descended from a monkey, that's for sure. No, sir. You'll be saying next that we have tails.'

'That's right,' said Smith, 'if you read the books you'll see that we have the remains of tails. And I'll tell you something else, what use is your appendix to you, tell me that.'

'My appendix,' said my uncle, 'what are you talking about? What's my appendix got to do with it?' And he winked at me in a conspiratorial manner as if to say, Listen to that hogwash.

'It's like this,' said Smith, who was a small intense man. 'Your appendix is no use to you. It's part of what you were as an ape. That's what the books tell you. You could lose your appendix and nothing would happen to you. You don't need it. That's been proved.' His wife smiled at Donalda and at me as if to say, They go on like this all the time but below it all they like each other.

'A lot of baloney,' said my uncle, 'that's what it is, a lot of baloney. When did you ever see a man turning into a monkey?'

'It's the other way round,' said Smith tolerantly. 'Anyway the time involved is too great. Millions of years, millions and millions of years.'

'Baloney,' said my uncle again. 'You read too many books, that's what's wrong with you. You'd be better looking after your garden. His garden is a mess,' he said, turning to me. 'Never seen anything like it. All he does is read and read.'

'And all you do is grow cherries and give them to widows,' said Smith chortling. 'Did you know that,' he said to me, 'he's surrounded by widows. They come from everywhere: they're like the bees. And he grows cherries and gives them baskets of them. Did you see the contraption he's got to keep the crows away from the cherry trees?' And he laughed.

Donalda and I looked at each other. My uncle had a wire which he strung out through the window of the kitchen and on it hung a lot of cans and a big hat and when he saw any crows approaching he pulled at the wire and the cans set up a jangling noise.

'They're like the Free Church ministers, them crows,' said Smith, 'you can't keep them away from the cherries.'

My uncle once told us a story. 'When I came here first I used to drive a cab and I used to take a lot of them ministers around to conferences. And, do you know, they never invited me into any of their houses once? They would leave me sitting in the cab to freeze. That's right enough.'

'All that baloney about monkeys,' said my uncle again. 'That's because he's got hair on his chest. Mind you, he does look a bit like a monkey,' he said to me judiciously.

Smith got angry. 'You're an ignorant man,' he said. 'Just because you were on the Fire Brigade you think you know everything. Do you know what he reads?' he said to me. 'He reads the *Fishing News* and the *Scottish Magazine*. He never read a book in his life. You wouldn't understand Darwin,' he said to my uncle, 'not in a million years.'

'And who's Darwin when he's at home?' said my uncle.

'Darwin?' Smith spluttered. 'Darwin is the man who wrote *The Origin of Species*. You're really ignorant. If you kept away from the widows you would know these things.'

'Do you think the widows are descended from the apes?' said my uncle innocently.

'Of course they are, and so are you.' Smith was dancing up and down with rage in spite of his limp.

'I never heard such hogwash,' said my uncle. 'Tell me something then. Do you swing from the trees in your garden instead of digging?' And he went off into a roar of laughter.

'Oh, what's the use of talking to you,' said Smith, 'no use at all. You're ignorant.'

And so the debate went on, though deep down we could see there was a real affection between the two men. When we were going home in the car my uncle would suddenly burst into a roar of laughter and say, 'Descended from the apes. Do you think Smith looks like an ape? Eh?' And he would laugh again. 'Mind you, where he comes from on the island they could be apes. Sure.' And he laughed delightedly again.

He was really rather boyish. He was always saying 'By golly', in a tone of wonder.

'Did you know,' he told us once, 'there's a woman here who comes from the island and her son-in-law is an ambassador. If you go to their house you'll find that the children have a room of their own with a billiard table and a television and everything else. And she sits there and makes scones as we used to do in the old days. You'd think she was back in Lewis. And when the kids come in, she says, "How much money did you spend today? Did you buy Seven Up?" And if they spent more than they should have, she gives them hell. And I once saw a millionaire in her house. Sure. He was walking along the corridor with a towel round him, he had been for a bathe, and that was all he was wearing. "That's a millionaire," she said to me. "That fellow?" I said. "Yes, that's right," she said. And he looked just like you or me. He said "Hi" to me as he passed. And there was water dripping all over the floor and all he was wearing was a towel.'

He had bought himself a cine camera and the last time he had been home to the islands he had taken some photographs. He showed us them one night and we saw figures of old women in black, churches, rocks, peat cutters, all flashing past at what seemed a hundred miles an hour. 'There's something dang wrong with that camera,' he muttered. Donalda and I could hardly keep from laughing.

All the time we stayed with him – which was three weeks – he wouldn't let us pay for anything. 'I won't be long for this world,' he would say, 'so I might as well spend my money.' And we fed on salmon and cherries and the best of steaks. And sometimes we would sit out in the garden wearing green peaked caps and watching the crows as they hovered around the cherry trees.

'When my wife was taken to hospital,' he said, 'I went to the doctor and I said to him, "No drugs. No drugs," I said to him. We never had a quarrel in our lives, do you know that? She was a great gardener. When we went out fishing on Sunday she would say, "Stop the car," and I would stop, though I drove very fast in them days, and it was a little flower she had seen at the side of the road.' He smiled nostalgically.

'This is my country now, you understand. I go back to the old country, but it's not the same. I've been to see the people who grew up with me, but they're all in the cemeteries. Sure. There was a schoolmaster we had and he used to go into a rage and whip us on the bare legs with a belt. Girls and boys, it was the same to him. But there's no one left now. Canada is my country now.' And he would look out the window at the men in red helmets who were repairing the road in front of his house.

The days were monotonously sunny. There was no sign of rain or storm. It was like being in the Garden of Eden, guiltless and without questions.

The night before we left many of the widows visited him, as did Smith and his wife. The widows brought scones, cakes, and buns, and made the coffee while he sat in the middle of the living-room like a king on a throne.

One widow said, 'You know what Torquil here said to my husband when he was building our house. He said to him, "I used to go duck shooting here when I came here first. It was a swamp."'

'And so it was,' said Torquil, laughing.

'He used to tell us, "The men here die young. The women live for ever. What they do is sell their houses and then they buy apartments in Vancouver."'

Another of the widows said to me, 'I saw one of your Highland singers on the TV. He had lovely knees.' All the other widows laughed. 'Lovely knees,' she repeated. And then she asked me if I knew the words of 'Loch Lomond'.

'Iain doesn't like that song,' said my uncle, largely. 'The fact is he despises them songs.' They gazed at me in wonderment. 'Iain doesn't like Burns either. But I'll tell you something about Burns. They say he had a lot of illegitimate children, but that was a lie put out by the Catholics.' He spoke with amazing confidence, and I saw Smith looking at him.

'I went home to Lewis,' said one of the women. 'The shop girls were very rude. I couldn't believe it.'

'Is that right?' said my uncle.

'As true as I'm sitting here,' said the woman.

Another one said, 'You've got lovely cherries this year.'

'Sure,' said my uncle, 'they're like the apples in the Garden of Eden.'

Smith suddenly pounced. He had been sitting on the edge of the company, brooding for a long time.

'It doesn't say that in the Bible at all.'

'What?' said my uncle, 'of course it says that.'

'Not at all,' said Smith, 'not at all. It doesn't mention the fruit at all.'

'I beg your pardon,' said my uncle, 'it says about apples as clear as anything. Do you know,' he said, turning to the widows, 'I read the Bible every year from end to end. I know the names of all the tribes of Israel. The gipsies, you know, were one of the tribes of Israel.'

'It doesn't say that at all,' said Smith, 'not at all. You read your Bible and it doesn't say it was an apple. It doesn't name the fruit at all.'

'What does it matter?' said one of the widows.

'We all know it was a woman who ate the fruit,' said my uncle magisterially.

'It might even have been a widow,' said one of the women. And the others laughed, but Smith didn't laugh. He was muttering to himself, 'It doesn't mention the fruit at all.'

'Next thing you'll be saying it was a pair of monkeys in the Garden of Eden,' said my uncle. 'You'll be saying it was the apes who ate the apple.' And he laughed so hard that I thought he was going to have apoplexy.

'Do you have a Bible here?' said Smith apologetically.

'I can't find it just now,' said my uncle.

I myself couldn't remember what it said in Genesis. My uncle started on a story about how once he had seen a black bear and it was eating berries in Alaska. 'They're very fast, you know,' he said. 'You'd think they would be slow but by golly they're not. By golly they're not.'

Some of the widows asked us if we were enjoying our holiday and we said, 'Yes, very much.'

'That's because Torquil is driving them about,' said one of the widows. 'He's a demon driver, did you know that? His wife used to shout at him and she was the only person he would ever slow down for.'

What did I think of Canada, I asked myself. There were no noises there, no creakings as from an old house. The indifferent level light fell on it. It was like the Garden of Eden uninfected by history. It was without evil. Smith was still muttering to himself. His wife was smiling.

'My friend here,' said my uncle largely, 'believes in the apes, you know. He thinks that we're all apes, every one of us.'

The women in their fine dresses and ornaments all laughed. Who could be further from apes than they were?

'Apes don't make as good scones as this,' said my uncle. 'Do you think apes make scones?' he asked Smith.

Smith scowled at him. He was looking around the room as if searching for a Bible.

'But there's one thing about John here,' said my uncle, 'by golly he's got principles. Yes by golly, he has.'

As the evening progressed we did sing 'Loch Lomond',

'... where me and my true love will never meet again
    on the bonny banks of Loch Lomond.'
I saw tears in my uncle's eyes.

'Mary was from Loch Lomondside,' said my uncle, 'but I couldn't find the house she was brought up in. She was an orphan, you know. Iain and I went there in the car but we couldn't find the house.' There was a silence.

'The only person he would ever obey was Mary,' said one of the widows.

'Gosh, that's right,' said my uncle. And then, it seemed quite irrelevantly, 'When I came here first we used to teach Gaelic to the Red Indians. Out of the Bible. And they taught us some Indian, but I've forgotten the words now. They spoke Gaelic as you would find it in the Old Testament. Of course some men used to marry squaws and take them home to Lewis. They would smoke pipes, you know.'

Smith was still staring at him resentfully.

At about one in the morning they all left. The night was mild and the women seemed to float about the garden in their dresses. My uncle filled baskets of cherries for them in the bright moonlight.

'That's the same moon as shines over Lewis,' he said. 'The moon of the ripening of the barley.'

They were like ghosts in the yellow light, the golden light. I thought of early prospectors prospecting for gold in the Yukon.

'You mark my words, you're wrong about that,' said my uncle to Smith as he pressed a basket of cherries on him. They all drove off to a chorus of farewells from myself and Donalda.

After they had gone, I looked up Genesis. Smith was right enough. It doesn't mention the particular fruit.

At the airport my uncle shook us by the hand briefly and turned away and drove off. I knew why he had done that. I imagined him driving to an empty house. Actually I never saw him again. He died the following year from an embolism. He dropped dead quickly in one of the bathrooms of a big hospital in Vancouver. He firmly believed that he would meet Mary again when he died.

The plane rose into the sky. Shadows were lying like sheaves of black corn on the Canadian earth which was not ours. It was still the same mild changeless weather. I hoped he wouldn't look up the Bible when he arrived home for he prided himself on his knowledge of it, and it was true that he read it from end to end in the course of a year. Even the tribes he memorized. And in the fly leaf of the big Bible were the names of his family and ancestors, all those who had passed it on to him.

I recalled the men in red helmets working in front of the house. He would drive in carefully. Then he would back into the garage and take off his glasses and walk into the house. Sometimes one could see grass snakes at the door sleeping in the sun, and Donalda had been quite frightened of them. One day my uncle had hung one of them round his neck like a necklace. 'You see,' he said, 'it's quite harmless. Sure. Nothing to fear from them at all.' At that moment the camera in my mind stopped with that image. The snake was round his throat like a green necklace, a green innocent Canadian ornament.

Mac an t-Sronaich

THE student saw Mac an t-Sronaich crouched by the fire at the far end of the cave.

'Of course,' said Mac an t-Sronaich, 'I am going to kill you.'

The student, who studied divinity and who had been on his way across the moor after a long journey, was frightened. Mac an t-Sronaich was wild-looking, had matted hair and a long nose. There had been stories of the murders he had committed and so far he had not been caught. He moved from cave to cave on the desolate moor and lived, it was said, partly on human and partly on animal flesh. After being sentenced for a crime on the mainland he had escaped and had sworn eternal enmity against society. The student trembled. He was tall and strong but looked pale.

'I am going to kill you,' said Mac an t-Sronaich, 'because there is nothing else for it. You've seen my cave. You will tell others.'

His red gibbering face glared from the smoke. He piled wood on the fire. He looked like a devil which had once haunted the student's dreams. God knew how he existed.

'Also I could do with some of your clothes. My own are in rags.' And he studied the student carefully.

'I can't believe it,' thought the student, 'I can't. I have travelled from Edinburgh, from the divinity college there, and here I am on this moor in the grip of a madman.'

He knew that Mac an t-Sronaich was a madman, though he talked rationally enough. How could one live like this and not be a madman? He knew that if he tried to run Mac an t-Sronaich would outrun him, at least the way he felt at the moment. And in any case it had been late evening when he had crossed the landscape of rocks and grass. Mac an t-Sronaich's eyes would be keener than his: they would find him in the dark.

Mac an t-Sronaich came and sat beside him, his big hooked nose prominent in his red face. The student recoiled from the smell which had something of fish in it, something of sweat, and something else unnameable. He looked strong as a bull, his flesh peering from among his rags like a moon through clouds. He wished to talk before he killed him. But then lonely men did wish to talk. The murderer was starved of conversation as he was often of food.

'Why should I not kill you?' said Mac an t-Sronaich. 'Tell me that.'

The student was paralysed with fear. He couldn't speak. It was like seeing a cat coming home triumphantly with a mouse between its teeth. Mice lived in such a world and so did cats. When they were eating they always looked around them in case they too were being stalked. The student had never imagined a world like this. To be killed like a mouse. To face that natural brutality.

'I see you are well-dressed,' said Mac an t-Sronaich, as if he were taking part in an ordinary conversation. 'No one has accused you of a crime and condemned you. Do you know what it is like to live here? The snow, the rain. The search for food. The traps. I have even eaten wild cat. Did you know that? Have you ever seen a wild cat? It's a terrible animal.'

The student couldn't think of a reason why Mac an t-Sronaich couldn't kill him if he wanted. Mac an t-Sronaich was studying his flesh as if tasting its sweetness in advance. He had heard of cases where human bodies were hung up like the carcasses of pigs.

'The Bible,' he muttered, trembling.

'The Bible,' said Mac an t-Sronaich, snorting contemptuously. And he made a sudden grab for the student's bag. He removed the sandwiches of bread and cheese and began to wolf them ravenously. He lived on the edge of the world.

Sometimes he might approach a village at night and kill a hen or a cockerel. Once he had even managed to drag a dead sheep away into the darkness. He was the murderer who lived on the circumference of lights and warmth.

The student could actually foresee Mac an t-Sronaich leaping at him. He could feel his hands on his throat, he could smell his stink. His own body flowed like water. He wished more than anything to be back in the warm room in the college listening to a lecture. The world of glosses, analysis, seemed far away. His books stood up in front of him. The voice of the lecturer droned like a bee.

Should he get down on his knees to pray for mercy? Should he plead for his life like a slave? And yet some pride made him not do it. What was the origin of that pride? And what was the origin of the idea that God had betrayed him? He had followed in His footsteps and now here he was in a smoke-filled cave like hell on the edge of a moor. It was crazy. It was beyond reality, logic. And then on the other hand he had nothing to bribe Mac an t-Sronaich with, no money. He had spent his last money on his journey home. Even now his parents would be waiting for him – his father was also a minister – in the halo of the lamp. And here he was in this cave face to face with a madman. The light of the fire made disturbing enigmatic patterns on the walls of the cave. An insane gibberish. And yet Mac an t-Sronaich sounded so reasonable.

'Don't think you can run away,' said Mac an t-Sronaich. 'I can run very fast. I've had to. You are my prey,' he said. And when he heard the word 'prey' the student again had a clear image of a cat and a mouse. He felt his whole body naked and vulnerable as if his clothes had been peeled from his skin. For this, he thought, I have followed the teaching of the Lord, for this I have been peaceable, tried to be without sin, though that is not possible, formed myself in His pattern. I have never drunk alcohol, never smoked. I have remained a virgin till the time for marriage comes. He saw his father's head bent over the big Bible inscribed with the names of his own father and mother. He himself sat upright in his pew gazing up at his father every Sunday. The face was bell-cheeked, red, healthy.

'I see you're a student,' said Mac an t-Sronaich at last. 'You have books in your bag.'

'Yes, I am,' said the student, trying to keep his voice under control. He felt that his teeth were chattering in his head. He was aware of his bones, of his flesh, of the blood pouring through his body. Indeed the place looked like the product of a man's fever, monstrous, dreamlike. He pinched himself in the stomach to find if it was a dream or reality. It was more like a dream that he had once had, a dream of a place from which he could not escape, with a white figure confronting him, smiling. And behind the white figure was his bearded father. For some reason he was dressed in a butcher's smock.

Let me die, he thought, let my heart give way. I can feel it beating heavily. But I don't wish to be killed in the smoke and the dark.

'I've thought about things a lot,' said Mac an t-Sronaich. Incredibly, he was now smoking a pipe. 'To kill or be killed, that is the rule of the universe. You can see it everywhere. Sometimes we kill by the mind, sometimes by the body.' He puffed out chains of smoke which were lost in the half darkness. 'You live off me with your nice clothes. At one time I never thought I would kill anyone. The idea would have been abhorrent to me. But I did. For money and food. On this very moor. It didn't bother me as much as I had expected. Not at all. After all, what use was the man to the world: there are so many people alive. What use are you? Does it matter whether you live or die? The victory goes to the strong. That's what your Christ didn't understand. He poisoned the world, made us all into pale-faced women.' And he spat on to the floor. 'But I am not a woman. I see the deer in the summer-time fighting each other, locking antlers, and they die like that, locked together. Men attack each other too. I know you are frightened but you needn't be. It won't last long, I promise you. And you have knowledge, you see, you have knowledge of my cave. I can't let you go away with that. When I killed that first man he evacuated everything in his body. What a stink! But then when you look at a dead body it is like a log. It has no light in it. You see I'm on the edge of things here. But I hear things. Sometimes at night I listen at windows to the quarrels between husband and wife, quarrels to the death. I have seen children who are eaten up with desire of possessions. I have heard businessmen (you find businessmen too in villages) making false deals in the darkness. I have listened outside these cages. It is as if they are inhabited by animals. That's where I get my entertainment from. I've eaten food in their kitchens while they are in their beds. I've crept in and out of their houses. And I have thought to myself, at least I am more honest than they. Do you understand?'

The student didn't answer. The murderer puffed at his pipe. It was like being at a ceilidh in a village, two men talking together contentedly. Why, the murderer might suddenly burst into song.

'And then again,' the murderer continued, 'people marry and when they do so they are no longer what they were. They are frightened. They sit by the fire and wonder what will happen to them when their partner dies. But I have outfaced a wild cat. Have you seen a wild cat?' The words poured from him in a torrent: his red cheeks glowed in the twilight. 'A cornered wild cat. And all I had was my bare hands.' He pointed at scars on the right one. 'I killed it as it was standing on end and its teeth were bared. That was an adventure. When people marry they no longer have adventures. There are the children at first and they have to be protected, and when the children leave there is the fear of loneliness. Have you ever thought that all we do is based on fear? I fear no one. Not even death itself. I've often been close to death here with fever and cold. I've seen a rabbit in the mouth of a weasel, which is thin as a string. I'm not afraid of death. Don't you be afraid of death either,' he said, almost gently.

His voice seemed to lull the student. And he thought, Why should I die? This is injustice. I didn't harm this man. Never. And he felt again the unfairness of the universe. And perhaps it was then that he forsook his God. In that smoke-filled cave his eyes were stung.

But the implacable Mac an t-Sronaich talked on. It was as if he hadn't seen a human being for twenty years. He was like Robinson Crusoe who has found a ship with a sailor on it.

'And the mornings,' he was saying, 'you cannot imagine what they are like. The sun, the dews, the flowers. The sweetness. Why, there have been times when I rolled in the dew like a hare. I have been so filled with joy. Have you ever felt such joy?' Only in the Lord, thought the student, only in His worn body yellow as parchment. Only in the psalms, in the holiness of a church, its peace and stillness. Only then. That was joy.

Mac an t-Sronaich tapped his pipe casually. 'I don't suppose you have any tobacco,' he asked.

'No,' said the student, 'I'm sorry, I don't smoke.'

'It doesn't matter. I can always steal some. People here often leave their doors open. It's amazing. They don't wish to admit that I can destroy their way of life. They want to hang on to it. They don't like to admit that I am different from them, that I can live without them.'

Suddenly the student was filled with anger. Why should this man kill me, he thought. I have never thought about it all till tonight.

Well, yes, I did hear of him. My mother especially warned me about him. She would say, Take your milk and go to sleep or Mac an t-Sronaich will get you. So Mac an t-Sronaich must really be quite old. The anger poured through the student's body like wine. Who does this murderer think he is? That he can rampage about this moor and kill anyone he likes. He looked around the twilit cave for a log but could see nothing he could use as a weapon. He felt his muscles tense. After all, he was not weak. He had thrown the javelin at the sports. He was in good shape, he had never drunk or smoked. Now he would have to fight for his life.

Better now while this holy anger possessed him before it drained away. Later, his body might be like water again.

He stood up.

'Where are you going?' said Mac an t-Sronaich.

'I am going away,' said the student.

'So that is what you are at?' Mac an t-Sronaich carefully tamped the fire in his pipe and advanced. It looked as if he had been doing this for years, advancing through the smoke with his red cheeks glowing.

'I cannot let you go,' he said to the student. 'You know that.' His beard was long and tangled, the muscles on his arms were huge. He put out his arms slowly. His eyes were on fire in the dark. The student stepped back. And then they were grappling with each other in the smoke that tingled and sparked.

It was the first time that the student had ever struggled with anyone. The arms of the monstrous murderer were about him, squeezing him, he was losing his breath. And then the most amazing thought came to him. Why, this is like love. This struggle is like love. Murder itself is like love. It is as if the cat is in love with the mouse as it flings the body up in the air, as it devours it, leaving violet-coloured intestines. He struck the arms away from him, and seized Mac an t-Sronaich by the throat with the frenzy of self-preservation. In order to save himself he had to be like Mac an t-Sronaich. He must empty his mind of books, ideas, become naked and pure.

'I shall not be killed,' he shouted aloud, 'I shall not be killed. I refuse to be killed.' And his voice echoed back to him.

And this extraordinary love that was involved in death almost overwhelmed him. Their legs were locked together but he would not let Mac an t-Sronaich's throat go. No, that was what he must cling to, the throat of this man who was not so young after all as he had been. Why, he must have been on the edge of that moor for years listening, mocking. He squeezed and squeezed. Mac an t-Sronaich managed to unlock his hands from his throat. He retched for a while and before he could recover himself the student was on him like a wild cat. He kicked him with his heavy boot right in the stomach. Then he jumped on top of him and held him by the throat again.

'I will kill you,' he shouted, 'I will kill you.' Never, never, had he thought he would be like this. Energies of the most astonishing kind flowed through him. Whose were these bell-shaped cheeks glaring up at him? His body was behaving with a logic of its own. Let him stop thinking, leave it all to his body, that was the secret. The long tangled beard thrust at him. He pushed the mouth slowly away from him with his hand.

This was the devil he had always wanted to kill, the devil that had tormented him, in the summer nights. Here he was in front of him, not abstract but concrete. He kicked again with his boot. Then he ran away into the darkness outside. He trembled in the silence watching the mouth of the cave. But no one came out. Instead he heard an insane laugh, and then a voice.

'Good for you, my friend.' The voice seemed to echo and echo. Yes, he thought, I will sit and watch the cave mouth till I see a shadow across it. He fumbled around him in the dark and found a big stone. He heard the secret mutterings of the night. I must not fall asleep, he thought, I must not fall asleep. And so he watched the flickering mouth of the cave. But no one came out. Instead he heard snoring as if Mac an t-Sronaich had fallen asleep or perhaps he was just pretending.

If only I had a wall that I could keep between him and me, he thought, feeling at his torn clothes. He held his breath till eventually the dawn came up red and angry. All night he had stayed awake. Then when the light bloomed he ran as fast as he could across the moor. He knew after a while that Mac an t-Sronaich would never catch him. And yet he kept seeing him, following him at a distance, sometimes on his left, sometimes on his right, sometimes even ahead of him. The mouth was full of broken teeth, he cast a salty smell on the air, there were coils of worms about his body. The fire shone like the fires of hell. Sometimes the moor itself seemed to disappear and he was back in his room at the college or he was at home and his father's head was bent over the table, bearded and still as if carved from stone. And the voice of Mac an t-Sronaich screamed at him as he ran and ran. And his body was infected with rage and shame. Bestially the dawn glared around him. There were clouds like red hot cinders in the sky. The dew arose around him smokily. There were red flowers like wounds growing from between the stones.

Oh God, he thought, this world will never be the same again. I shall never return to my college now that I have, like the mouse against the cat, fought in my grey nakedness. He was like a white vulnerable root, which had finally been tugged out of the earth.

My God, he shouted from the bare moor, but no answer came from the sky. His voice hammered against it with a metallic sound. And then in the distance like an echo he seemed to hear the voice of Mac an t-Sronaich. And he saw again the enigmatic whirlings of the smoke in the cave. He knew that Mac an t-Sronaich was not dead and would never die. Even among the fog and lights of gas-lit Glasgow he might meet him. Even in his own house. Even in his own mirror.

I Do Not Wish to Leave

IN the thatched house the fire was in the middle of the floor and they sat on benches around it in the smoke. There were six people altogether. This was the ceilidh house in the village, the one where on certain nights there was a gathering to tell stories, sing songs, sometimes play music. This was a tradition in the Highlands in the old days.

The host was called Squashy. At one time he used to be a shoemaker: now he was retired. He would sit by the wall watching the world go past, for his legs were very bad with arthritis, and he could walk only with the help of two sticks. He had never left the island in his life but he read a fair amount and thought that he knew more than he did. His favourite reading was about Egypt and the pyramids, the burials of the Pharaohs in big tombs which had been prepared by slaves, the murders of servants, the voyage of the king-god across the sky.

He was not married and lived with his sister. She had been at one time a servant on the mainland in a hotel but she was also rather simple-minded and wore stockings which accordioned down to her ankles. She deferred to her brother even though he had seen less of the world than she had. He treated her with contempt.

He was in fact speaking at that moment, saying '... and do you know that they had mummies in those days. My sister here Mary doesn't know what a mummy is but the rest of us do, don't we? They used to take the bodies and make them into mummies, that's what they did in those days.'

'What did they treat them with, eh?' asked Cum, who was a big fat man wearing a fisherman's jersey. He was engaged in building his own house and had been so for years. He had a thin daughter with very thin legs who would meet the boys on Sunday among the corn.

'I don't know what they treated them with, I wasn't there, was I?' said Squashy shortly. 'But it was something mysterious, you can depend on that.' He shifted his bottom on the hard wooden seat. 'They were very clever people and what they put in their heads they put in their feet.' And he looked significantly at Cum with his small, angry red eyes as if implying, They would have finished your house years ago.

'That's true, it would have been something mysterious,' said Shonachan. Shonachan was perhaps forty years old. He came from an odd family who hardly ever left the house. There were seven of them altogether and he was the only gregarious one. The others would sit at windows gazing out on to the road: one in particular was shouted at and laughed at by the local children and he would shake his fist at them from behind the curtains. One sat in a corner of the house endlessly repairing fishing nets as if he were a spider. Shonachan found relief in his visits to the ceilidh house.

'And another thing,' said Squashy, leaning back against the white-washed wall, 'another thing. They buried them deep in tombs so that no one would ever find them. And people tried to rob the tombs but they got lost among the passages and they were never found again.'

The others thought of this among the swirling smoke of the fire, their faces shining, for all of them believed in ghosts and mysterious events: why, there was supposed to be a ghost at the corner of the road. And also Alastair Macleod had seen a ghost the last time he was home from his work on the mainland and shortly afterwards he had died. Ghosts were not to be taken lightly. The fire shone on their faces and they imagined the false passages and the robbers lost among them.

'That may be true,' said John Smith consideringly. Curiously enough he had never been given a nickname by the villagers. He was the scribe who used to write their letters for them if they were at all official, and he would show them the letters, and they would all think what a clever man he was. 'Dear Sirs,' he would write, 'thank you for yours of the 21st inst.' Imagine that, the 21st inst. He had also been to America and he had many stories and had at times picked Squashy up on a number of points. But Squashy was like an eel in a river, difficult to catch.

'That may be true,' said John Smith. He looked around him with a judicial air. 'That may be true,' he repeated. Only he gave the impression that he didn't believe it.

'Of course it's true,' said Squashy, 'it's all in the books.' His books coloured the air around him with a foreign radiance and John Smith stared at him as if saying, 'Well, for the moment I will let you away with this. Many things happen in this world and I have seen them myself, having been to America, while you haven't been out of the island.'

Squashy continued, 'And another thing. The cat was their god and that's another thing that you find out. They wouldn't allow anyone to do anything to a cat.'

The sixth person, who was called Pat and who was also the local postman, listened carefully. Cats, eh, what was this about cats? Dogs perhaps, but not cats. Nothing had happened so far this night and he was comfortable, almost sleepy. But nevertheless the others were wary of him because of his reputation. Sometimes he thought that they would prefer if he didn't attend their ceilidhs. But being alone in the house he sometimes felt the need of company and he couldn't prevent himself from coming. It wasn't his fault that he was as he was. It was inheritance, it had been in his people. It was a sorrow and a triumph, that's what it was.

The cat glared at him from his seat beside the fire.

Oh, God, let me have peace, he thought, let it not happen tonight.

'The cat,' said Squashy, 'that was what they worshipped.'
'Imagine that, the cat,' said his sister.
Cum thought, One of these days I'll finish my house. My

wife wants it finished. And yet the other day when I was shifting that big stone I felt a twinge. It's still there.

Pat listened. He enjoyed being in this social ring, damned though he was. He loved the glitter of the fire, the voices, the stories. Why, one day he would like to visit those pyramids in the desert.

'There's a lot we don't know about right enough,' said Shonachan. He dreaded going back to the house where the hearth was often cold. He wished they had a housekeeper. And he was smoking far too many cigarettes. One of these days he would have to give them up or they would kill him. Full strength Capstans. In the mornings he coughed and coughed and spat and spat and he fought for breath and his chest ached. But what could he do?

With regard to yours, thought John Smith, with regard to yours, I have to tell you...

They don't know, thought Squashy, what my life is like sitting by the wall in the heat or the cold, my hands turning red round the sticks, thinking, thinking... Why did this have to happen to me? And this stupid sister of mine as well. That is another cross I have to bear. They don't know the length of my days and without Egypt where would I be? His little moustache quivered with self-pity.

And then it happened to Pat, they could all see it happening. He stood up and as if in a dream walked to the door through the smoke which loomed and drifted around him. Just like that it happened. Again. And he was frightened. Oh, he was frightened, but he was also compelled. From that warm circle, that ring of smoke and fire, he went out into the frosty night, for it was freezing heavily and the stars were clearly visible in the sky, twinkling and sparkling.

And they watched him with fear but they did not try to stop him. It was almost as if his eyes were closed. Then the door shut behind him and they were left alone.

There was a silence and no one looked at his neighbour. It was as if a dreadful death had fallen over the ceilidh house and they were all suspended in their individuality, like statues of Pharaoh.

Finally Shonachan spoke, 'Who is it this time?' he said. No one answered. All they knew was that it was one of them. And for a moment they felt mortal and cold in front of the fire as if death were at their breasts. Like stony effigies they sat there.

Pat went out into the night. The stars were twinkling and the ground was hard. He walked as if in a trance. There was no sound to be heard and the earth like an enchanted stone rang under his feet. How brilliant the sky was, so many stars like a huge city, each one answering the other in a brave bright language.

And then he saw them. They were coming from his left, the men in hard hats walking slowly. And they were carrying a coffin. He waited for them to come. The coffin was open and he could see the face. The funeral party walked slowly: it did not even stop at the stream. The stream was crossed, with the coffin. Pat's trousers were wet: he could feel the water making them heavy. They made their way towards the cemetery, taking short cuts, and all the time he could see the face in the coffin.

They laid the coffin down. There was a prayer, and after a while he turned back, walking again through the stream, opened the door of the ceilidh house, and entered. This was his sorrow and his triumph. They were all silent looking at him. They noticed the wet trousers and knew that it happened again. His eyes travelled over them like a light as if he were saying, I know you, I have power over you. But he did not speak and they did not ask any questions. They were vexed in their mortal individualism around the sociable fire. Death had come into the room. Each looked at Pat and thought, Is it me, is it me? But Pat gave no sign. He never did. He never passed his final judgment.

And the ceilidh broke up and they all went home.

Pat loved being a postman. He loved bringing letters to people who hadn't heard from their sons or daughters for years before. What a surprise, what a joy! He would never like to live anywhere else than where he lived. Why, when he was on his rounds, the birds would be singing in the sky, the stones glittered, the sun shone, red and brilliant. No one saw the world as he did carrying his bag around the village. The dew glittered, the trees bore their blossoms, and in the bag were the signs of hope, communications from the whole wide world. And now and again he would stop at a house and have a cup of tea and narrate the gossip that he had picked up. No, he could not live anywhere else. He had been to other villages but this was his favourite. He had never married, so attractive was his work and his life. Apart of course from that other shadow.

And if he were to marry would he gaze down one morning at the pillow beside his own and see death imprinted on the face of his wife. And perhaps one day he would even see his own face in the coffin. How could one know?

He walked on. A bare tree was reflected in the loch. In the summer its berries were like open wounds. Oh, how beautiful the day was, even though he carried his mysterious knowledge around with him. And that too was power, was it not? Of a sort. He knew, he knew...

John Smith took the letter from him and thought, I wonder if it's me. He studied Pat's face, but it was open and cheerful as usual. It can't be me then, thought John Smith. Otherwise how could he be so cheerful. Maybe I should propitiate him, ask him in for a cup of tea. On the other hand, he suddenly hated him. Why should he have been given that power? It was wrong, it was unhealthy, and it wasn't as if he was intelligent. And he glanced at his letter. It was about the croft, he could tell that right away.

Cum watched him from the roof of the incomplete house where he perched like a cockerel. Maybe I'll never finish it. That stone is in my breast. I may have injured myself. I may be dying at this very moment. Who knows? But I do know that the others look down on me, I know that. But if I don't finish this house what will my wife say? He hammered, and made no sign that he had seen Pat. He completely ignored him. He wouldn't speak to him. You are not going to tell me when I'm going to die, my friend. I have my rights too.

Shonachan didn't see him, for he was working away from the village, but Squashy watched him from the wall where he sat like an owl thinking about Egypt. His hands were red and glassy in the cold. Pat waved to him but he made no acknowledgement. You bugger, he thought, you're like a vulture, you perch on the bones of men. Was it his own bell-like moustached face that Pat had seen in the coffin? Should he shout to Pat and ask him? But he didn't, he had too much pride. After all, what was Pat but an incomer from another village, and there were stories... In fact he had been in many villages, that was a fact. He rested on his sticks like a wounded proud Pharaoh.

It might be me, thought his sister. And to tell the truth she didn't care. No one knew what it was like living with her brother with his mocking ways. It seemed to the outside world as if he coped well with his ailment but she knew he didn't. He was always complaining about little things. There wasn't enough salt in his porridge, not enough sugar in his tea. She wouldn't be unhappy if suddenly...

And Pat passed on less cheerfully. Something glacial, something frosty, had entered the air. Was it going to happen again as it had happened before? Some cold air was blowing towards him.

He humped his bag over his shoulder. What a glorious quiet frosty morning, so clear, so calm. Such a holy day. But he knew that face in the coffin and the knowledge was his grief and his pride. Some tried to bribe him, others not. Some had bribed him to tell, if they thought they would inherit money.

'Please tell me, Pat, is it Jim? The old monster. He's so mean.' And Pat would remain tight-lipped except that twice, twice only, he had released himself from his burden and the man had died. But was it destiny that had killed him or the revelation? Who could tell? And so Pat was like a crow traversing the countryside.

No, they will not drive me out, not again.

One fine morning, as fine as any he had known, they were waiting for him. Cum, Shonachan, John Smith. The three of them.

They were standing in front of a gate through which he must pass on his round. They were frowning and hostile.

He tried to pass but they stood in his way.

Cum spoke first. 'Who is it?' he said.

Pat said, 'I can't tell. I am not supposed to tell. You know that.'

'You had better tell,' said Shonachan. For a man usually so calm he was aggressive. He wasn't smoking as many cigarettes as he had done.

'You'd better tell,' said John Smith.

But, no, he would not tell. He had made this mistake before and he would not do it again. No, he would not do it again. It was his secret. And the very telling might be the death blow.

'If you don't tell,' said Shonachan, 'you will have to leave and that's the end of it. We will not have you in the village.' The phantom taste of cigarettes bothered him.

So this was it happening again. It always happened. Always. And up to now he had never learnt. No one wanted a death-dealer in their village.

He stared at Cum, the bag over his shoulder. His red face shone in the day from the effort of carrying his letters and parcels.

Now he must make a new effort. He did not wish to leave. Not again. It was too late. He was getting old and he wanted to stay where he was. But to give birth to the monster, that was bad, for he knew that it might be the monster that killed.

The three of them stood in front of him: Shonachan with his slightly greying hair, John Smith like a civil servant, with his clever eyes, Cum, huge as the side of a house in his fisherman's jersey. It was a moment of tremendous silence.

He laid his bag down gently on the ground. If he told, what would happen? Would they attack him, would they drive him out just the same into the other villages. But he did not wish to go. All that was over for him. He would face them out this time, it was his own life that he was saving.

He thought for a long time and then he pointed at Cum, and he saw Cum's face disintegrating in front of him. 'You forced me to tell,' he shouted. Cum seemed to fall apart like the house he had never completed. His face quivered like a child's.

And then amazingly he saw the other two withdrawing from Cum, as if in horror, and turning ever so slightly towards himself.

The moment passed, he was safe.

The hostility had left the faces of Shonachan and John Smith. Indeed it was as if the three of them, these two and Pat himself, formed a new ring.

And they watched as Cum stumbled away from them like a wounded sheep.

'It's terrible,' said Shonachan, searching for his cigarettes.

'Awful,' said John Smith. And then to Pat, 'You saw him?'

'Yes,' said Pat, 'as clearly as I see you.' Much more clearly than anyone had seen the Pharaoh's mummy.

And yet and yet... In the service of death itself what could one do? To defend onself? Knowing all of them...

'Yes,' he said, 'I saw him as clearly as I see you.'

The land around them became fresh and beautiful again. Shonachan saw it through the smoke of his cigarette. For Pat it was his joy and his triumph resurrected. No one would ever again drive him from it. He had done with his exile.

And in front of him as it were he saw Cum like the Pharaoh travelling through the sky like a god, huge and eternal, while John Smith was writing. Thank you for yours of the 14th inst. I have to tell you that after due consideration and much thought I have come to the conclusion that... The pen hung over the page. His clever eyes would never tire. But above him travelled the heavy, wounded, puzzled Pharaoh, his unfinished pyramid below him in the desert.

The Ghost

I

IT was a bleak windy evening when they arrived at the hotel, situated by itself at the roadside with the bare moor behind and around it, he the artist and she the wife. At first they weren't sure whether the hotel was open, since it was still cold January, but in fact it was, and when through driving rain they ran to the door and pressed the bell a tall youngish man in tweeds appeared and told them that they could have bed and breakfast. They took the cases in from the car in silence and signed the register while the tweeded man who they thought was the owner agreed that the weather was grim, and, yes, he could provide them with a drink and, yes, they could have dinner.

They went into the lounge where there was a paraffin heater, black leather seats, and on the walls a number of landscapes which the artist glanced at with some contempt, for he himself painted in the modern style, that is to say, abstractly. They sat in silence staring at the heater: there was no one but themselves in the lounge.

Sheila the wife didn't speak: she knew that the holiday had been a disaster but she was unwilling to take the blame. Her husband looked at her now and again as if about to say something and then changed his mind. Even after the stormy crossing on the boat her blonde hair was carefully combed, her suit impeccable. He looked out of the window at the sea which was still tempestuous and restless, white waves foaming round the rocks.

They sipped their whiskies and sat in silence. Who would have thought that she would have turned out to be so religious and intolerant and dark? It was a part of her nature that hadn't shown clearly in Edinburgh. And as for himself, he hadn't realized that such places existed, such intolerant boring dull places where time oozed like treacle, where people would sit for hours staring into the fire, where the fear of death was everywhere, where life had been pared to the minimum, where his red velvet jacket blazed out of the grey monochrome like a scarlet sin. His head still felt as if it had been flayed.

'It was a bit of a disaster,' he said frankly, turning towards her.

'I thought you would say that,' she answered, and turned away again.

To tell the truth she had been frightened by the sight of her own true nature, concealed for so long in Edinburgh. And yet it was her nature and it had to be reckoned with.

'All those elders and ministers,' he said, 'those endless graces. I couldn't even show them my paintings. Imagine that. They thought they were idols and the work of the devil, they really thought that.' He truly didn't understand them, not at all. His own upbringing – free and sophisticated – hadn't prepared him for that darkness, that constriction.

'I felt,' he said, 'as if someone was squeezing me slowly to death.'

'I was brought up there,' she said, sipping her whisky very carefully as if she were already thinking of giving it up, and all this after a fortnight.

'I know,' he said. 'I hadn't realized . . .' And then he stopped.

'Hadn't realized what?'

'How much of you belongs to that island. How you accepted it all, how clearly you are one of them.'

'I hadn't realized it myself,' she said. Of course they had only been married six months but even so, not to have known . . .

'But do you not see,' she insisted, 'that in a way they are right?'

'Right!'

'Their lives are ordered,' she said. 'They have order.'

So that was what she was looking for. Order. Certainly he couldn't give her that, not that sort of order. That sort of death.

'I felt so secure,' she said. 'All the time I felt so secure.'

After your chaotic life, she meant. After your terrifying disorder.

'They know where they are going,' she said. 'Where we are all going.'

Her blonde composed head turned towards him passionately. 'Don't you see? They are preparing. They are readying themselves.'

'For death,' he answered, seeing so clearly the black shawls around the breasts like black shields, the wind stropping the bare windy moor.

'The lack of colour,' he mused. 'That was the worst of all. Nothing but black and white. Nothing but sorrow and sighing. Nothing but fear. They are frightened to live.'

She was about to reply when the tweedy man came back in and said that they could have their food now. They followed him into the large deserted dining-room.

'Would you like some wine?' he asked her.

'No, thanks.'

'Well, I'll take some,' and he ordered a German wine that he had never heard of before.

They sat facing each other alone in the dining-room which had more landscapes on the walls. The island had almost killed him, it was only now that he was beginning to waken up. He wanted a theatre of the body, music, joy, colour. But she didn't want any of these things. It was as if she had returned to an aboriginal guilt on which she was feeding in silence as a trembling shorn Eve suddenly feels frightened of the apple in her hand, bitten and in such a short moment discoloured. He had a picture in his mind of the scoured streets of the island town, of the men and women in black, of the salt piercing wind, of the churches and cemeteries, of the barrenness and the blackness, of the psalms rising and falling like the sound of the sea.

Of her father saying grace, of the truisms endlessly delivered as if they were revelations from God. 'We are so hard-hearted,' he would say, 'there is no good in us.' He had felt as if he must free Sheila from a demonic world. But she had lowered her head like a cow about to be axed, and surrendered herself to that world as if returning to her helpless childhood again.

'Will steak do?' said the tweedy man. Steak would do. They ate in silence.

The two worlds – that bare one and the world of the artist – hung around them like contrary paintings. He felt as if he might never paint again. An old woman struggling against that eternal wind of death in her black clothes, that was what he might paint, nothing joyful. He felt tired to the bones and she was staring down at her plate. It was almost as if she expected him to say grace. The vanity. She had even stopped using perfume.

'I'm not saying anything against your people,' he said.

She looked up questioningly.

'But,' he said, 'God did not mean us to be like that. Surely he didn't.'

'How do you mean?' she asked, her eyes very blue and cold and distant.

'I felt as if I was being squeezed to death. It is not right to feel like that.'

'Aren't we all being squeezed to death?' she said. And yet in earlier days she had been so gay and happy. Perhaps too much so, he thought now, perhaps with too much desperation.

On their holiday they had met an alcoholic who lived alone and whose room was filled with empty bottles. But no one asked him why he had become an alcoholic. Everyone avoided him, they made no allowances for the temptations and the terrors. No one questioned himself, no one asked, 'Am I my brother's keeper?' He shuddered. And even now as he looked out of the window he could see the bareness and the storm and the rain lashing the ground, with its grey whips. Inside the house there was the wine on the table. He drank some more while she looked at him disapprovingly, though she said nothing.

He felt his hands clench as if around a paint-brush that could no longer paint pictures.

He felt as if he were fighting against some form of possession, possession by God. So many days they had sat by the fire, gazing into it as if into a mirror which showed scenes from the past, the dog asleep on the floor and now and again twitching in its sleep, the clock ticking, time devouring them. Ships on the stormy seas, bringing letters from America, from Australia, from the exiles.

He was suffering from culture shock. He remembered his own upbringing, the playing of the piano in the large sunny drawing-room, the reading of novels, the endless simple unprincipled traffic of the world. The art galleries. On the island he was the stranger, the enemy. No one would look at his pictures.

So much of what we do is vain, she said. And she was so beautiful, that was what was so heartbreaking. But the island would destroy her beauty, it would eat her alive, it would put shapeless clothes round her infernal breast. He drank some more wine. He wanted to get drunk, to forget about the cemeteries, the cold hard wind.

They had some trifle after the steak and he drank some more wine.

'This is quite an old hotel,' she said, 'really. They've modernized it. That's all.'

'Yes, perhaps you're right. And we're the only guests here.'

If only she would dance as she had used to do. But now he could see that her former frenzy had been an escape from herself, from the darkness. From that incessant flaying wind, from that devilish music.

'Don't you see?' she said eagerly. 'They have adapted. They have adapted to the bareness. There's no protection. Not even in art. Nothing protects us from mortality.'

'And all your – their – lives,' he said, 'they are preparing for death.'

'Yes,' she replied. 'It is another way of seeing the world. Perhaps it is the true way, without deception.'

'No,' he said, flushed with the wine. 'I won't allow it to be. It can't be. I want the vanity, the unpredictability, the perfumes, the mirrors.'

She flinched as if he had struck her. He drank some more wine. The tweedy man came in and asked if they would have tea or coffee. They would have coffee. He paused for a moment and told them that it was worthwhile keeping the hotel open in the winter because of the bar trade, that life here was very different from life in the south, that he hadn't begun to live till he came here. He shot and fished and boated. The artist fancied that he looked now and again at Sheila who, however, stared straight ahead of her. Her faithfulness mirrored his own. For a moment he thought that religion would make her even more loyal, more predictable and he felt contentment but not joy. A large dog came into the room and gazed at them with large tranquil eyes. Fidelity. Peace.

When they had had their coffee they sat a little longer and then Sheila said that she wished to go to bed, though it was still quite early. They climbed the stairs together and he fitted the key in the lock of the door. As he went in he had an impression of glass, another door perhaps at the end of the corridor. In the room itself there were twin beds, an oldish dressing table with a large spotty mirror, a wardrobe, and an electric fire which looked broken. He tried to fit some coins into the slot but failed. They undressed in silence, took their chill night-clothes from their cases and went to bed. He noticed that she was wearing a long chaste nightgown which he couldn't remember having seen before: perhaps it was an heirloom which had been given her when she was home. He stayed awake for some time staring up at the ceiling and then, feeling quite tired, fell asleep.

II

He woke up in the middle of the night and groped for the light to see what time it was. It was three o'clock.

'What are you doing?' said Sheila.

'I'm sorry,' he said, 'I didn't realize you were awake. It's three o'clock. Didn't you sleep?'

'Yes, I slept,' she said irritably. For some reason he had an impulse to be teasing and provocative and he said, 'Imagine. Suppose there's a ghost in the hotel.'

'What?'

'A ghost.' And then more daringly. 'Suppose we two are ghosts. Suppose the real you has gone out while I was sleeping and you are a ghost.'

'What nonsense.'

'But think of it,' he said. 'How do I know that you're not a ghost? How do you know that I'm not a ghost? How do you know that the real me hasn't gone out and that only my spirit is here?'

But he wasn't able to frighten her though he was almost frightening himself. All round the hotel on that desolate moor there might be ghosts shimmering in their long white chaste nightgowns. For a moment he really thought that perhaps she was a ghost as he listened to her breathing, a bed away in the darkness. If the two of them were ghosts, if time had changed during their sleep, in this room so old and dim with the ancient furniture!

What women had sat at that mirror who were now in all corners of the world or dead? What women or men had slept in these very beds and had wakened perhaps at three in the morning and had spoken to each other as they were speaking now? He felt himself sweating and wanted to put the light on again. Perhaps if he did so he would only see a skull lying on the bed next to him. But he was too frightened to switch it on and lay awake staring at the ceiling which he couldn't see. Hotels, how strange they were. Transients of all kinds passed through them, the old and the young, the sane and the insane, the crippled and the healthy. They all lay down in those beds and slept in them. They woke in the early hours of the morning and lit cigarettes and thought about their lives, wasted or fruitful.

'It's true,' he said in a whisper across the dark space, 'we could be spirits.'

'Oh shut up,' she said. And then she got up and switched the light on. 'I have to go to the bathroom.'

'All right,' he said, grateful for the light.

He watched her as she walked across the floor to the door. She was really very beautiful with her blonde hair streaming down her back. One would never have suspected that she had succumbed to the powers of darkness – or the powers of light. She pulled the door behind her and he was left alone again. All round him was absolute silence, the silence, he thought fearfully, of the grave itself. What if she never came back? What if she disappeared forever? What evidence would there be that she had ever been with him, if the tweedy fellow was involved in some ghostly complicated plot.

But she did come back, shutting the door behind her and saying excitedly: 'What an extraordinary thing.'

'What's so extraordinary?' he said.

'You know that glass door down at the end of the corridor,' she said, 'well, there was a woman standing behind it. She wore a black shawl and she looked quite old. Must be the owner's mother.'

'Funny,' he said.

'Yes,' she said, 'perhaps she can't sleep. She didn't look spooky or anything. I only had a glimpse of her. Maybe there's another bathroom over there, the family quarters perhaps, and she was going to or coming back from the bathroom.'

'I suppose so,' he said.

'I'm sure she can't sleep,' said Sheila. 'That's what it is. She was looking at me and then I had an impression of her turning away.'

'Perhaps you'd better lock the door anyway,' he said.

'All right,' she said, 'is that better?'

'Fine.'

'Well in that case,' said Sheila, 'I'd better get to sleep and so had you. You've a lot of driving to do tomorrow morning.'

'Okay,' he said. 'What did she look like?'

'Oh, just an old woman with a black shawl. She looked a bit hunchbacked. That was all. I don't know what you're going on about her for. The curious thing was that she looked vaguely familiar. Maybe I caught a glimpse of her in the hotel tonight without realizing that I'd seen her.'

'It's possible,' he said.

Now that the door was locked he felt quite secure. He turned over on his side and almost immediately fell asleep.

He was awakened by the sunlight falling across the bed and into his eyes. Sheila was already up and sitting in front of the mirror tidying herself. He himself felt joyful and light hearted as he often did on a sunny morning, aware of a new unused world opening before him, alive with hope and cheerfulness. When he got up he went behind her and put his arms around her. She shrank away from him, not much, but enough for him to notice.

'Don't be a clown,' she said, 'put on your clothes. You'll be cold.'

He did his Groucho Marx walk across the room as he had often done on the island while walking along the street, wondering if anyone would notice. But in fact no one had looked at him: perhaps they really thought he was a cripple.

'Oh, oh, oh,' he sighed heavily, imitating her father and glancing at her mischievously. But she didn't react in any way and only looked into the mirror searching for signs of approaching age. That, he thought, was good: at least she hadn't forgotten she was a woman. He padded round her, the sex fiend of the Highlands. 'An inconspicuous elderly man with a wooden leg and a mask has been taken into custody,' he intoned, 'for the murder of an old woman who had inflicted psalms on him for fifty years. Pleading justification the man said that she had a rotten voice anyway.' She didn't smile at first but then gradually did. He was happy again.

'I think,' he said in his normal voice, 'that we should take our cases down with us. Save us coming back to the room again after breakfast.'

'All right,' she said.

So they packed their night-clothes in their cases and walked along the corridor, he behind her.

He didn't know what made him turn as he was leaving the door of the bedroom behind him but in any event he did turn. He stared directly towards the glass door at the end of the corridor and saw with horror, quite clearly, himself and his case, and she slightly ahead of him with her own case also reflected in it. As he moved and looked backwards the image moved with him.

With horror such as he had never known he realized that what he was looking at was not a glass door at all but a mirror.

His head spun but he had enough presence of mind to nudge her forward as she was about to turn and look at him. In that case (his spinning brain was telling him) what she had seen was not an old woman in black at the far end of a glass door but herself walking towards the mirror. And the vague sense she had of the woman turning away was herself turning in at the bedroom door.

She went into the bathroom on her way downstairs and he waited outside it, ready to prevent her for any reason from walking back along that corridor towards what she had thought was a glass door but what was in actual fact a mirror.

And as he sat there on a chair conveniently provided outside the bathroom the world turned round and round and finally came to a stop and he saw her as she would be in the future, old and clad in black exactly like that woman whom he had thought of painting as she breasted the sharp island wind. He stared straight ahead of him at a painting on the wall which showed a hill and a loch and a boat and its amateurishness seemed to gather about it like a black shadow descending from the badly drawn sky.

When she came out of the bathroom he picked up the case and walked down the stairs, she ahead of him. When the tweedy man asked them if they had slept well he said that they had. He wished to be away as soon as possible, ate little, and when his wife was about to ask about an old woman who might or might not live in the hotel he quickly sent the man off to make out the account for bed and breakfast.

Behind the wheel of the car, later, he drove at seventy miles an hour for mile on mile. Disapprovingly she sat beside him but said nothing. For a good part of the way he found himself looking in the mirror to see if there was anything following them but all he could see was a small yellow car with a small man in glasses at the wheel who was staring ahead of him unsmilingly. Beside him was his taller wife and behind both of them there sat upright a tall black dog which gazed ahead of it with an air of tranquil ownership.

On the Island

THEY tied up the boat and landed on the island, on a fine blowy blue and white day. They walked along among sheep and cows, who raised their heads curiously as they passed, then incuriously lowered them again.

They came to a monument dedicated to a sea captain who had sailed the first steam ship past the island.

'A good man,' said Allan, peering through his glasses.

'A fine man,' said Donny. 'A fine, generous man.'

'Indeed so,' said William.

They looked across towards the grey granite buildings of the town and from them turned their eyes to the waving seaweed, whose green seemed to be reflected in Donny's jersey.

'It's good to be away from the rat race,' said Donny, standing with his hands on his lapels. 'It is indeed good to be inhaling the salt breezes, the odoriferous ozone, to be blest by every stray zephyr that blows. Have you a fag?' he asked Allan, who gave him one from a battered packet.

'I sent away for a catalogue recently,' said William. 'For ten thousand coupons I could have had a paint sprayer. I calculate I would have to smoke for fifty years to get that paint sprayer.'

'A laudable life time's work,' said Donny.

Allan laughed, a high falsetto laugh and added,

'Or you might have the whole family smoking, including your granny and grandfather, if any. Children, naturally, should start young.'

The grass leaned at an angle in the drive of the wind.

'We could have played jazz,' said William, 'if I had brought my record player. Portable, naturally. Not to be plugged in to any rock. We could have listened to Ella Fitzgerald accompanied by her friend Louis Armstrong who sings atrociously, incidentally.'

'Or, on the other hand, we could have played Scottish Dance Music each day. "The Hen's March to the Midden" would not be unsuitable. I remember,' he continued reflectively, keeping his arms hooked in his lapels, 'I remember hearing that famous work or opus. It was many years ago. Ah, those happy days. When hens were hens and middens were middens. Not easy now to get a midden of quality. A genuine first class midden as midden.'

'The midden in itself,' said William. He continued, 'The thing in itself is an interesting question. I visualize Hegel in a German plane dropping silver paper to confuse the radar of the British philosophical school, and flying past, unharmed, unshot, uncorrupted.'

'I once read some Hegel,' said Allan proudly, 'and also Karl Marx.'

Donny made a face at a cow.

They made their way across the island and came to a pillbox used in the Second World War.

'Sieg Heil,' said William.

'Ve vill destroy zese English svine,' said Donny.

'Up periscope,' said Allan.

The island was very bare, no sign of habitation to be seen, just rocks and grass.

'Boom, boom, boom,' said Donny, imitating radio music. 'The Hunting of the Bismarck. Boom, boom, boom. It was a cold blustery day, and the telegraphist was sitting at his telegraph thinking of his wife and four children back in Yorkshire. Tap, tap, tap. Sir, Bismarck has blown the Hood out of the water. Unfair, really, sir. Bismarck carries too strong plating. Boom, boom, boom. Calm voice: "I think it'll have to be Force L, wouldn't you say, commander?" And now the hunt is on, boom, boom, boom, grey mist, Atlantic approaches, Bismarck captain speaks: "I vill not return, herr lieutenant.

And I vill not tolerate insubordination." Boom, boom, boom.'

William looked at the pillbox, resting his right elbow on it.

'I wonder what they were defending,' he mused.

'The undying right to insert Celtic footnotes,' said Donny.

Allan said,

'I was reading a book about Stalingrad. You've got to hand it to these slab-faced Russians.'

The wind patrolled the silence. The green grass leaned all one way. There were speedboats out in the water plunging and rising, prows high.

'Oh well, let us proceed, let us explore,' said William. As they were walking along they came to a seagull's ravaged body, the skull delicate and fragile, lying among some yellow flowers. The carcass had been gnawed, probably by rats. Its white purity in the cold wind was startling. Its death was one kind of death, thought William with a shudder. Suddenly he placed the seagull's fragile skull on top of a hillock, and they began to throw stones at it. Donny stood upright, one hand clutching a stone, the other still in his lapel.

'Have I been successful?' he asked, after he had thrown the stone.

Allan went over. 'No,' he said shortly and took up position. In a frenzy, William threw stone after stone, but missed. It was Allan who finally knocked the seagull's skull from the knoll.

'All these years, like David, watching the sheep,' he admitted modestly.

They walked on and came to the edge of the water on the far side of the island. They were confronted by a seething waste, tumbled rocks, a long gloomy beach, a desert of blue and white ridged waves, a manic wilderness. As they stared into the hostile sea they saw a boat being rowed past by a man with a long white beard who sat in it very upright as if carved from stone. It was very strange and eerie because the man didn't turn his head at all and didn't seem to have noticed them. Donny broke the silence with,

'Ossian, I presume.'

'Or Columba,' said Allan.

'Once,' said Allan, 'I was entertaining two friends.'

'Ladies,' they both shouted.

'Let that be as it may,' said Allan, 'and may it be as it may. I, after the fourth whisky, looked out the window and there, to my astonishment, was a blanket, white with a border of black stripes, waving about in the air. I need not say that I was alarmed; nor did I draw the attention of the two people I was entertaining to it; nor did they notice it. At first, naturally, I thought it was the D.Ts. But better counsels prevailed, and I thereupon came to the conclusion that it must be the woman above engaged in some domestic activity which entailed the hanging of a blanket out of her window.'

'It was,' said Donny, 'the flag of the Scottish Republic, a blanket with...' He stopped as the bearded man rowed back the way he had come. They watched the white hair stirred in the cold wind and the man with his upright stance.

'The horrible man,' said William suddenly.

'The thing in itself,' said Donny.

'Scotland the Brave,' said Allan, cleaning his glasses carefully. 'I remember now,' said Donny. 'I saw these two green branches on a tree and, full of leaves, they were dancing about in a breeze just outside my window. I didn't pay any attention to them at first and then I saw that they were like two duellists butting at each other and then withdrawing, like, say scorpions or snakes, upright, as if boxing. Such venom,' he concluded, 'in the green day.'

He added, 'Another time I was coming home from a dance in a condition of advanced merriment and I was crossing the square, all yellow, as you will know. Thus I came upon a policeman whom I had often seen in sunny daylight. He asked me what I was doing, looking at the shop window, and I returned a short if suitable answer, whereupon he, and his buddy who materialized out of the yellow light like a fairy with a diced cap, rushed me expeditiously up a close and beat me furiously with what is known in the trade as a rubber truncheon. It was,' he concluded, 'an eye opener.'

'Once,' said William, 'I saw a horse and it could think. It was looking at me in a calculating way. I got out of there. It was in a field on a cold day.'

They stared in silence at the spray, shivering.

'There is a man who is supposed to live in a cave,' said William at last. 'It must be an odd existence.'

'Mussels,' said Donny.

'Whelks,' said Allan.

'All locked up for the night,' said William.

After a pause he said,

'Nevertheless, it's got to be faced.'

'What?' said the others.

'This wilderness. Seas, rocks, animosity, ferocity. These waves all hating us, gnashing their white teeth.'

'I think,' said Allan, 'we should do a Socrates.'

'Meaning?' said Donny.

'Meaning nothing. Irony is not enough any more.'

'It's the inhumanness,' said William, almost in a whisper, feeling what he could not say, that for the waves they themselves didn't matter at all, any more than the whelks or the mussels.

Donny stood facing the water, his hands at his lapels. 'Ladies and gentlemen,' he began, 'Mr Chairman, ladies and gentlemen, guests, hangers-on, attendants, servants, serfs, and tribesmen, I have a few words to say about a revered member of our banking profession: well-known bowler, bridge-player, account-keeper, not to mention the husband of a blushing bride who looks as good as new after clearing her fiftieth hurdle.'

'You're right,' said Allan. 'He's right you know, Willie.'

'Meaning?'

'He faces it. He faces the chaos. Without dreams, without chaos. Only without chaos is it possible to survive. The plant does not fight itself, neither the tiger nor the platypus.'

'You mean that that speech orders the waves,' said William. 'Let me think.'

After a while he said,

If thou didst ever hold me in thy heart,
absent thee from felicity awhile
and in this harsh world draw thy breath in pain
to tell my story.

'They have their purpose and their eyes are bright with it. Keats.'

'Meaning?' said Allan.

'Meaning vanity. If there were no vanity there would be nothing. The flowers and the women all drawing attention to themselves. The signals. Have you not known, have you not seen, all the people around you, each with his own purpose staring out of his eyes and proclaiming "I am." "I am the most important. Look at me." "I must not be trifled with"? Have you not known it, have you not seen it, have you not been terrified by it? That each feels himself as important as you, that intelligence weakens, that the unkillable survive, the ones who don't think?'

A seagull swooped out of the stormy black and landed on a rock with yellow splayed claws, turning its head rapidly this way and that as if deliberating.

'Then,' said Donny, 'vanity prevails.'

'Without vanity we are nothing,' said William, 'without the sense of triumph.'

'And we have to pay for it with pomp,' said Allan. 'Out of the savage sea the perfected ennui.'

'From the amoeba to the cravat,' said Donny. The wind blew about them: it was like being at the end of the world, the crazy jigsaw of rocks, the sea solid in its strata, the massive power of its onrush, the spray rising high in the sky.

'Where action ends thought begins,' said William, almost in a whisper. 'Out of the water to the dais. And yet it is unbearable.'

'We rely on the toilers of the night,' said Donny.

'Is there anything one can say to the sea,' said Allan, 'apart from watch it?'

They looked at it but their hatred was not so great as its,

not so indifferent. It was without mercy because it did not know of them. It was the world before man.

'Imagine it,' said William, 'out of this, all that we have.'

'And us,' said Donny, no longer clowning.

'To watch it,' said Allan. After a while he said,

'It would be fair if we threw stones at it too.'

'Yes,' agreed the other two, beginning to throw stones at the white teeth, but they sank without trace and could hardly be seen against the spray which ascended like a crazy ladder.

There was no ship to be seen at all, only the weird rowing boat that had passed twice with the white bearded man in it.

They turned away from it, frightened.

As they were leaving, Allan said,

'There is nothing more beautiful than a woman when her long legs are seen, tanned and lovely, as she drinks her whisky or vodka as the case may be.'

They bowed their heads. 'You have found the answer, O spectacled sage of the west. Except that the battle there too is continuous.'

'Except that everywhere the battle is continuous,' said William. 'Even in the least suspected places. But you are right nevertheless.'

They took one last look at the sea. In the smoky spray they seemed to see a fish woman, cold and yet incredibly ardent, arising with merciless scales.

'I knew a girl once,' said Allan. 'We slept on the sofa in her sitting-room.'

'Both of you?' said the others.

There was a reverent silence.

'I knew a girl once,' said William. 'I remember her gloved hands on the steering wheel, and the dashboard light was green.'

Their clothes stirred in the breeze. Their flapping collars stung their cheeks. They passed the place where the dead sea-gull was.

'We will bury it,' said Allan. 'It's only fair.'

'No,' said William, 'it would be artificial.'

'Agreed,' said Donny. 'Motion carried, seconded, transformed and retransformed in some order.'

They saw a rat. It looked at them with small beady eyes and scurried out of sight.

'Look,' said William. A cormorant dived from a rock into the seething water. They watched for it to emerge and then it did so like a wheel turning. Also, they saw three seals racing alongside each other at full speed, sleek heads and parts of the body above the surface.

'They say it is the fastest fish in the sea,' said William.

'They say seals turn into women,' said Allan, polishing his glasses. They watched the speedboats drilling through the water. The town with its spires, halls, houses, pubs, rose from the edge of the sea, holding out against the wind. It was what there was of it. Nothing that was not unintelligible could be said about it.

Home

THE black polished car drew up outside the brown tenement and he rested for a moment, his hands still on the wheel. He was a big man with a weatherbeaten red-veined face and a strong jaw. On one finger of his right hand was a square red ring. He looked both competent and hard.

After a while he got out, gazing round him up at the sky with a hungry look as if he were scanning the veldt. His wife, in furs, got out more slowly. Her face had a haggard brownness like that of a desiccated gipsy and seemed to be held together, like a lacy bag, with wrinkles.

He glanced up at the tenement with the cheerful animation of one who had left it, and yet with a certain curiosity.

'Lock the car, dear,' said his wife.

He stared at her for a moment in surprise and then said as if he had been listening to a witticism, 'But they don't steal things here.'

She smiled disdainfully.

They walked into the close whose walls were brown above, and a dirty blue below, and pitted with scars. Somebody had written in chalk the words YA BASS. It looked for a moment African, and he stared at it as if it recalled some memory.

From the other side of the road the flat-faced shops looked back at them blankly.

He pointed upwards towards a window.

'Do you mind the Jamiesons?' he said.

She remembered them but took no pleasure in the memory.

The Jamiesons lived above them and were Protestant. Not

68

that at that level you could distinguish Catholic from Protestant except that the former went to chapel and the latter didn't go to any church at all. The O'Rahillys' house – for instance – had been full of wee ornaments, and once she had seen a complete ornamental house, showing outside it, like Europeans on a veranda, Christ and the twelve disciples, the whole thing painted a distasteful green.

She remembered Jamieson all right. Every Friday night he would dress up in his best blue suit, neat as a ray or razor, and wave to his wife who was following his progress to the road from an open window, her scarf tight around her head. He would go off to the pub, and pick a fight with a Catholic, or more likely three Catholics. At midnight he would come home covered with blood, his face bruised a fine Protestant blue, his clothes dirty and brown. He would strut like a victorious gladiator up the stair and start a fight with his wife, uprooting chairs and wardrobes till the silence of exhaustion settled over the flats at about one in the morning. The next day his wife would descend the stair, her eyes black and blue, and say that she had stumbled at the sink. Her repertoire of invention was endless.

'I remember,' she said.

The town had changed a lot since they had left it, that much was clear. The old tenements were being knocked down and the people shuttled out to huge featureless estates where the windows revealed at night the blue sky of TV. There were hardly any picture-houses left: they had been converted into bingo-halls. Instead of small shops, supermarkets were springing up, flexing their large muscles. The lovers' lane had disappeared. The park seemed to have lost its atmosphere of pastoral carelessness and was being decorated with literate slogans in flowers.

'It's thirty-five years since we left,' said her husband.

And the wallet bulged from his breast pocket. A wife, two children, and a good job in administration.

He moved about restlessly. He wanted to tell someone how well he had done but how could he do that? All the people he had known were gone elsewhere, many of them presumably dead, and completely forgotten.

'Do you mind old Hannah?' he said.

She had been a fat old woman who sat day after day at the window, leaning out and talking to the passers-by. A fat woman with arthritis. He wondered vaguely what had happened to her.

'I wonder if the coal-house is still here. Come on.' He took his wife by the hand and they walked down the close to the back. The coal-houses were, incredibly, still there, all padlocked and beside each other, all with discoloured doors.

She kept her fur coat as far away from them as she could.

'Do you mind the day I went to see the factor?' he said. The factor had been a small, buttoned-up, black-suited lawyer. In those days of poverty he himself had been frightened to visit him in his tiny office with the dim glass door. He imagined what he would do to that factor now.

He had gone there after coming home from the office, and the lawyer in the undertaker's suit had said to him over his shoulder, 'What do you want?'

'I want to report the rain coming through the roof.'

'How much do you pay, Jackson?'

'Fifteen shillings a week.'

'And what do you expect for fifteen shillings a week?' said the factor, as if even giving away words were an agony of the spirit. In a corner of the office an umbrella dripped what seemed to be black rain.

'I wis hoping that the house would be dry anyway.'

'I'll send someone round tomorrow,' and the factor had bent down to study a ledger with a rusty red cover.

'You said that a week ago.'

'And I'm saying it again. I'm a busy man. I've got a lot to do.'

At that moment he had been filled with a terrible reckless anger and was about to raise his fist when the factor looked up. His mouth opened slightly, showing one gold tooth in the middle of the bottom row of teeth, and he said carefully, 'Next week.'

So he had walked out past the dispirited receptionist in the glass cage – she had a limp and an ageing mother – and had gone home.

Thinking back on it now, he mused savagely, I was treated like a black. That's what it amounted to. By God, like a black.

He wished that the factor was still alive, so that he could show him his bank balance. The wee nyaff. The Scottish words rose unbidden to his mouth like bile.

For a moment he did in fact see himself as a black, cringing in that rotting office, suffering the contempt, hearing the black rain dripping behind him from the furled umbrella.

But then a black would buy a bicycle and forget all about his humiliation. Blacks weren't like us.

As he turned away from the coal-house door he saw the washing hanging from the ropes on the green.

'You widna like to be daeing that noo,' he told his wife jocularly.

'What would the Bruces say if they saw you running about in this dirty place like a schoolboy,' she said coldly.

'Whit dae ye mean?'

'Simply what I said. There was no need to come here at all. Or do you want to take a photograph and show it to them, *The Place Where I Was Born*.'

'I wisna born here. I jist lived here for five years.'

'What would they think of you, I wonder.'

'I dinna give a damn about the Bruces,' he burst out, the veins on his forehead swelling. 'Whit's he but a doctor ony-way? I'm no ashamed of it. And, by God, why should you be ashamed of it? You werena brought up in a fine house either. You worked in a factory till I picked you up at yon dance.'

She turned away.

'Do you mind that night?' he said contritely. 'You were standing by the wa' and I said, Could I have the honour? And when we were coming hame we walked doon lovers' lane, where they had a' the seats an' the statues.'

'And you made a clown of yourself,' she said, unforgivingly.

'Yes, didn't I jist.' Remembering how he had climbed the statue in the moonlight to show off. From the top of it he could see the Clyde, the ships and the cranes.

'And remember the flicks,' he said. 'We used to get in wi jam jars. And do you mind the fella who used to come doon the passage and spray us wi disinfectant?'

The interior of the cinema came back to him in a warm flood: the children in the front rows keeping up a continual barrage of noise, the ushers trying to hush them, the smoke, the warmth, the pies slapping against faces on the screen, the carved cherubs in the flaking roof blowing their trumpets.

'You'd like that, wouldn't you?' she said. 'Remember it was me who drove you to the top.'

'Whit dae ye mean?' – like a bull wounded in the arena.

'You were lazy, that was what was wrong with you. You'd go out ferreting when you were here. You liked being with the boys.'

'Naething wrang wi that. Whit's wrang wi that?'

'What do you want? That they should all wave flags? That all the dirty boys and girls should line the street with banners five miles high? They don't give a damn about you, you know that. They're all dead and rotting and we should be back in Africa where we belong.'

He heard the voices round him. It was New Year's Eve and they were all dancing in a restaurant which had a fountain in the middle, and in the basin hundreds of pennies.

'Knees up, Mother Brown,' Jamieson was shouting to Hannah.

'You used to dance too, on New Year's Eve,' he said.

'I saw auld Manson dying in yon room,' he said, pointing at a window. The floor and the ceiling and the walls seemed to have drops of perspiration, and Manson had a brown flannel cloth wrapped round his neck. He could hardly breathe. And he himself could hear the mice scuttering in the walls.

She turned on him. 'What are you bringing that up for? Why don't you forget it? Do you enjoy thinking about these things?'

'Shut your gab,' he shouted. 'You didna even have proper table manners when I met you.'

She stalked out to the car and he stayed where he was. To hell with her. She couldn't drive anyway.

He just wondered if anyone they had known still remained. He climbed the stair quietly till he came to the door of their old flat. No gaslight there now. On the door was written the name 'Rafferty' and as he leaned down against the letter-box he heard the blast of a radio playing a pop song.

He descended the stair again quietly.

He thought of their own two rooms there once, the living-room with the table, the huge Victorian wardrobe which was too big for the bedroom, and the huge Victorian dresser.

As he looked out of the close he saw that his car was surrounded by a pack of children, his wife sheltered behind glass, staring ahead of her, an empress surrounded by prairie dogs.

He rushed out. 'Hey,' he said, 'don't you scratch my car.'

'What is it?' a hard voice shouted from above.

He looked up. 'Nothing,' he said. 'I was telling them not to scratch my car.'

'Why have you goat it there onyway?'

The woman was thin and stringy and wore a cheap necklace. A bit like Mrs Jamieson but less self-effacing.

'I was just paying a visit,' he said. 'I used to live here.'

'They're no daeing onything to your caur,' said the voice which was like a saw that would cut through steel for ever.

'It's an expensive car,' he said, watching his wife who was sitting in it like a graven image, lips firmly pressed together.

Another window opened. 'Hey, you there, I'm on night shift. Let's get a bit of sleep, right. Right?'

A pair of hairy hands slammed the window down again.

Two tall youngsters chewing gum approached.

'Hey, mister, whit are you on about?' They stared at him, legs crossed, delicate narrow shoes.

'Nice bus,' said the one with the long curving moustache. 'Nice bus, eh, Charley?'

They moved forward in concert, a ballet.

'Look,' he began, 'I was just visiting.' Then he stopped. Should he tell them that he was a rich man who had made good? It might not be advisable. One of them absently kicked one of the front tyres and then suddenly said to his wife, 'Peek a boo.' She showed no sign that she had seen him. They reminded him of some Africans he had seen, insolent young toughs, town-bred.

'All right, lads,' he said in an ingratiating voice. 'We're going anyway. We've seen all we want.'

'Did you hear that, Micky? He's seen all he wants to see. Would you say that was an insult?' Micky gazed benevolently at him through a lot of hair.

'Depends. What have you seen, daddy?'

'I used to live here,' he said jovially. 'In the old days. The best years of my life.' The words rang hollow between them.

'Hear that?' said Micky. 'Hear him? He's left us. Daddy's left us.'

He came up close and said quietly, 'Get out of here, daddy, before we cut you up, and take your camera and your bus with you. And your bag too. Right?'

The one with the curving moustache spat and said, quietly, 'Tourist.'

He got into the car beside his still unsmiling wife who was staring straight ahead of her. The car gathered speed and made its way down the main street. In the mirror he could see the brown tenement diminishing. The thin stringy woman was still at the window looking out, screaming at the children.

The shops along both sides of the street were all changed. There used to be a road down to the river and the lavatories, but he couldn't see one now. Later on, he passed a new yellow petrol station behind a miniature park with a blue bench on it.

'Mind we used to take the bus out here,' he said, looking towards the woods on their right where all the secret shadows were and the squirrels leaped.

The sky was darkening and the light seemed concentrated ahead of them in steely rays.

Suddenly he said, 'I wish to God we were home.'

His wife smiled for the first time. But he was still thinking
of the scarred tenement and of what he should have said to
these youths. Punks. He should have said, 'This is my home
too. More than yours. You're just passing through.'

Punks with Edwardian moustaches. By God, if they were
in Africa they would be sorted out. A word in the ear of the
local inspector over a cigar and that would be it. By God,
they knew how to deal with punks where he came from.

He thought of razor-suited Jamieson setting out on a Friday
night for his lone battle with the Catholics. Where was he
now? Used to be a boiler-man or something. By God, he
would have sorted them out.

'So you admit you were wrong,' said his wife.

He drove on, accelerating past a smaller car and blaring his
horn savagely. There was no space in this bloody country.
Everybody crowded together like rats. 'Here, look at that,'
he said. 'That didn't use to be there.' It was a big building,
probably a hospital.

'That didn't use to be there,' he repeated, almost sullenly.

He drove into the small town and got out of the car to
stretch. The yellow lights rayed the road and the cafés had
red globes above them. He could hardly recognize the place.

'We'd better find a hotel,' he said.

His wife's face brightened.

They stopped at the Admiral and were back home when
the boy in the blue uniform with the yellow edgings took
their rich brown leather cases. People could be seen drinking
in the bar which faced directly on to the street. They were
standing about with globes of brandy in their hands. He recognized who they were. They had red faces and red necks and
they stood there decisively as if they belonged there. Their
wives wore cool gowns and looked haggard and dissipated.

His own wife put her hand in his as they left the car. Now
she was smiling and trailing her fur coat negligently. She
walked with a certain exaggerated delicacy. It might be a good
evening after all. He could tell the boys about his sentimental
journey, an edited version, it would make a good talking point,

they would get some laughs from it. No, on second thoughts perhaps not. He'd make sure however that they got to know how well he had done in a foreign country.

The two of them walked in. 'Waiter,' he said, 'two whiskies with ice.'

Some of them looked at him, and then turned away again. That waiter should have his hair cut. After a few whiskies he and his wife would gravitate into the neighbourhood of the others, those men who ran Scotland, the backbone of the nation. People like himself. By God, less than him. He had had the guts to travel.

Outside it was quite dark. Difficult to get used to this climate. His wife was smiling as if expecting someone to photograph her.

Now she was home. In a place much like Africa, the bar of a first-class hotel. He took out a cigar to show who he was, and began to cut it. In the lights pouring out from the hotel he could just make out his car, bulging like a black wave.

He placed his hand over his wife's and said, 'Well, dear, it's been a tiring day.' With a piercing stab of pain he recalled Africa, the drinkers on the veranda, the sky large and open and protective, the place where one knew where one was, among Europeans like oneself.

To have found one's true home was important after all. He sniffed his whisky, swirling it around in the glass, golden and clear and thin and burningly pure.

The Dying

WHEN the breathing became worse he went into the adjacent room and got the copy of Dante. All that night and the night before he had been watching the dying though he didn't know it was a dying. The grey hairs around the head seemed to panic like the needle of a compass and the eyes, sometimes open, sometimes shut, seemed to be looking at him all the time. He had never seen a dying before. The breathlessness seemed a bit like asthma or bad bronchitis, ascending sometimes into a kind of whistling like a train leaving a station. The voice when it spoke was irritable and petulant. It wanted water, lots of water, milk, lots of milk, anything to quench the thirst and even then he didn't know it was a dying. The tongue seemed very cold as he fed it milk. It was cold and almost stiff. Once near midnight he saw the cheeks flare up and become swollen so that the eyes could hardly look over them. When a mirror was required to be brought she looked at it, moving her head restlessly this way and that. He knew that the swelling was a portent of some kind, a message from the outer darkness, an omen.

Outside, it was snowing steadily, the complex flakes weaving an unintelligible pattern. If he were to put the light out then that other light, as alien as that from a dead planet, the light of the moon itself, would enter the room, a sick glare, an almost abstract light. It would light the pages of the Dante which he needed now more than ever, it would cast over the poetry its hollow glare.

He opened the pages but they did not mean anything at all

since all the time he was looking at the face. The dying person was slipping away from him. She was absorbed in her dying and he did not understand what was happening. Dying was such an extraordinary thing, such a private thing. Sometimes he stretched out his hand and she clutched it, and he felt as if he were in a boat and she were in the dark water around it. And all the time the breathing was faster and faster as if something wanted to be away. The brow was cold but the mouth still wanted water. The body was restlessly turning, now on one side now on the other. It was steadily weakening. Something was at it and it was weakening.

In Thy Will is My Peace... The words from Dante swam into his mind. They seemed to swim out of the snow which was teeming beyond the window. He imagined the universe of Dante like a watch. The clock said five in the morning. He felt cold and the light was beginning to azure the window. The street outside was empty of people and traffic. There was no one alive in the world but himself. The lamps cast their glare over the street. They brooded over their own haloes all night.

When he looked again the whistling was changing to a rattling. He held one cold hand in his, locking it. The head fell back on the pillow, the mouth gaping wide like the mouth of a landed fish, the eyes staring irretrievably beyond him. The one-barred electric fire hummed in a corner of the room, a deep and raw red wound. His copy of Dante fell from his hand and lay on top of the red woollen rug at the side of the bed stained with milk and soup. He seemed to be on a space ship upside down and seeing coming towards him another space ship shaped like a black medieval helmet in all that azure. On board the space ship there was at least one man encased in a black rubber suit but he could not see the face. The man was busy either with a rope which he would fling to him or with a gun which he would fire at him. The figure seemed squat and alien like an Eskimo.

And all the while the window azured and the body was like a log, the mouth twisted where all the breath had left it. It lolled on one side of the pillow. Death was not dignified. A dead face showed the pain of its dying, what it had struggled through to become a log. He thought, weeping, this is the irretrievable centre where there is no foliage and no metaphor. At this time poetry is powerless. The body looked up at him blank as a stone with the twisted mouth. It belonged to no one that he had ever known.

The copy of Dante seemed to have fallen into an abyss. It was lying on the red rug as if in a fire. Yet he himself was so cold and numb. Suddenly he began to be shaken by tremors though his face remained cold and without movement. The alien azure light was growing steadily, mixed with the white glare of the snow. The landscape outside the window was not a human landscape. The body on the bed was not human.

The tears started to seep slowly from his eyes. In his right hand he found he was holding a small golden watch which he had picked up. He couldn't remember picking it up. He couldn't even hear its ticking. It was a delicate mechanism, small and golden. He held it up to his ear and the tears came, in the white and bluish glare. Through the tears he saw the watch and the copy of Dante lying on the red rug and beyond that again the log which seemed unchanging though it would change since everything changed.

And he knew that he himself would change though he could not think of it at the moment. He knew that he would change and the log would change and it was this which more than anything made him cry, to think of what the log had been once, a suffering body, a girl growing up and marrying and bearing children. It was so strange that the log could have been like that. It was so strange that the log had once been chequered like a draughtsboard, that it had called him into dinner, that it had been sleepless at night thinking of the future.

So strange was it, so irretrievable, that he was shaken as if by an earthquake of pathos and pity. He could not bring himself to look at the Dante; he could only stare at the log as if expecting that it would move or speak. But it did not. It was concerned only with itself. The twisted mouth as if still gasping for air made no promises and no concessions.

Slowly as he sat there he was aware of a hammering coming from outside the window and aware also of blue lightning flickering across the room. He had forgotten about the workshop. He walked over to the window and saw men with helmets bending over pure white flame. The blue flashes were cold and queer as if they came from another world. At the same time he heard unintelligible shoutings from the people involved in the work and saw a visored head turning to look behind it. Beyond it steadied the sharp azure of the morning. And in front of it he saw the drifting flakes of snow. He looked down at the Dante with his bruised face and felt the hammer blows slamming the lines together, making the universe, holding a world together where people shouted out of a blue light. And the hammer seemed to be beating the log into a vase, into marble, into flowers made of blue rock, into the hardest of metaphors.

The True Story of Sir Hector Macdonald

HE became Major General Hector Macdonald, he who had been brought up in the Black Isle in the Highlands of Scotland. Apprenticed at an early age to a shopkeeper in Inverness he ran away to join the army in Aberdeen. Sent to Afghanistan he was promoted rapidly, reaching the rank of Colour Sergeant: and after two episodes where he showed conspicuous bravery he was sent for by General Roberts who gave him the choice of a VC or a commission in the Gordon Highlanders.

'Better a commission in the Gordon Highlanders than to be a Member of Parliament,' said the impeccable soldier. Nor perhaps did he realize then that to hold a commission in peacetime in the Army of that day was to expose himself to expense that only a private income could cope with. And that to rise from the ranks to a commission was further to expose himself to humiliation and jealousy and envy.

And loneliness. Above all loneliness.

After the mountains of Afghanistan, after the bodies of the rebels had twisted slowly in the wind, he was ordered to South Africa to take part in the Boer War, a very different kind of war where the enemy were like ghosts, sharpshooters, brilliant amateurs.

At Majuba Rock he among others climbed at night to ensconce themselves above the Boer camp. Sliding about the rocks in hobnailed boots they entrenched themselves, digging wells for water. In the early morning one of the soldiers shouted to the sleeping Boers to come up and fight like men. There was a scrambling of Boers from their camp which became like a live anthill and then the rock became an inferno of heat and fire. As the British soldiers were picked off by the Boer sharpshooters the rock became a cauldron flowing with blood. Hector fought with his bare fists but was eventually overpowered, made prisoner, and had his sword taken from him. Later he was released and as a gesture of respect had his sword returned to him: the Boers recognized a brave enemy.

The First Boer War had however been a disaster.

Hector went to the Sudan to train native soldiers to fight the Dervishes. The Sirdar, called Kitchener, a hater of women, built a road along the Nile along which he sent his armour to avenge Khartoum. The desert was infested with flies but most beautiful at night with its millions of stars. From water-holes dead camels stared back at one. Kitchener's iron road drove undeviatingly for Omdurman, as he made his bullish rush at the enemy. The Mahmud was dragged behind a horse to pay for Gordon's death. Kitchener's army marched relentlessly forward supported by ships and big artillery. At night one could see the searchlights from the ships dividing the sky into sections. One could also hear the sleepless drums of the enemy. Maxims cut the Dervishes down and they lay like black sheaves while Kitchener made for Omdurman, not realizing that many more of the enemy were hidden behind sand dunes. Hector or Fighting Mac as he was called was surrounded by them. Cool as an icicle he told his men with the harsh fury of the ex-sergeant that they must wait till the enemy were close before they fired, and his trained Sudanese obeyed him. His army was outnumbered by ten to one and caught between two forces. At that moment he invented a spontaneous dance of march and countermarch, retreat, advance, retreat, advance, while sabres cut and drums beat till they heard the pipes of the Cameronians, and the Dervishes – thirty thousand of them at the beginning – began to break. Later it was said that it was Hector who by his coolness had given Kitchener his victory.

Promoted to Brigadier General he was made Commander of the Bath and an ADC to the Queen, while Kitchener was voted thirty thousand pounds by Parliament. Hector who needed the money was instead given ceremonial swords, banquets, freedom of cities. Highland societies acclaimed him – 'Pray silence for Colonel Macdonald.' The Earl of Kincardine, the Duke of Atholl, were among the guests at these dinners. He had been promoted dizzily from private to the rank of a high officer but he was still lonely, perhaps more so now that envy became acute. After all had he not been just a leader of black troops? And was it not his training as a sergeant that had drilled his force sufficiently to save the hour at Omdurman?

He begins to write to a young boy whom he had met in Aberdeen. Again he is sent to fight the Boers in charge of the Highland Brigade who were in disgrace because they had run away at Magersfontein after they had been propelled in darkness to make a frontal charge on entrenched Boers who picked them off like ducks. Six hundred men had been killed in a few minutes. Lord Methuen stood on a platform and told them, 'Your primary duty is to the Queen, then to your country, lastly to yourselves.'

Hector himself drills his troops in sections like a sergeant but is wounded in the foot at Modder River while his unprotected men advance, again under the overall charge of the unimaginative and bullish Kitchener. The war was a stinking abattoir, the enemy was a taunting lightning on the hills.

Hector is given the charge of some gentlemen Volunteers and rages at them in pain and frustration: why can't these Boers stand and fight like honest men? Kitchener invents his concentration camps and in spite of comparative failure caused by his wound and accumulated fatigue, Hector is knighted and sent to Australia, and New Zealand, and finally to Ceylon, a post suitable to tired old superannuated army horses. From the latter place he was ordered home after rumours of homosexual adventures, the sin of David and Jonathan.

Roberts, himself happily married, didn't understand the loneliness which led to the offence if offence it was. King Edward, bulbous-eyed womaniser, understood even less.

Hector was ordered back to Ceylon to face a jury of his peers. On his way there he stopped off at Paris where he took lodgings. One morning he went to buy a morning paper and there in the New York Herald found that the story about him had broken. He walked back to his lodgings and shot himself. His body was rushed hugger mugger to London in a plain coffin and from King's Cross was taken by train to Deans Graveyard where he was buried in a rainy grey dawn with only a few mourners present.

These then are the facts about this famous soldier, of whom it was said by grieving admirers that he was not dead, his coffin had been filled with stones, and that he was the Mackensen who fought in the German Army in the First World War.

In such speculation I am not interested. I have a speculation of my own. It is Paris, city of culture, of books and poems and opera, in the early morning, and Hector Macdonald is walking along one of its streets in search of a newspaper. He is the simple flower of the British Empire, he has fought for it till he has grown weary, he has been a good linguist, but not a cultured man in the Parisian manner. He has committed the sin of Sodom and Gomorrah and his home village is biblical and puritanical.

No, I am not concerned with any of that. On the contrary I am concerned to follow this man down the Parisian street in the early morning. I imagine it as early morning, pearly grey. There he walks, stiff-necked, ramrod-backed, this Highlander who has become a world figure: and I imagine, for one can imagine such things, passing him on the other side of the street a young painter called Picasso perhaps with a brush in his hand. And Hector does not notice him, and Picasso does not notice him either. And Picasso may be thinking of a collage of bits of newspaper stuck on a painting, and it may be that he will use the same newspaper which has just told of Hector's disgrace. At any rate they pass each other on this pearly morning, the old soldier who has fought for the Empire, the flawed lonely man who has climbed into the sky only to be brought down like a pheasant by jealous guns: and the painter with the eyes as piercing as twin gun barrels.

Two worlds let us imagine, one dying, one about to be born.

And then as if the image has been frozen it begins to move again, and there is the crack of a gun in the very heart of the Empire, creating eddies of disturbance, spreading outwards. The coffin is hurried north in a weeping dawn – the initials HAM written on it – and Picasso returns to his studio. It is a day in March at the beginning of the twentieth century.

Chagall's Return

WHEN I came home the cat was smiling and the walls of the house were shaking. The door opened and there was my mother in front of me.

'Who are you, my child?' she asked, and her eyes were unfocused and mad. There were other old women in black with her and they nodded to me over and over. I went to see a neighbour who was ploughing, and afterwards I took buckets to the well and brought in water. But my mother was still gazing at me with unfocused eyes and she asked me again and again who I was. I told her about the skyscrapers and the man with the violin, but she could understand nothing.

She kept saying, 'In the old days there were cows, and we were children. We would take them to the grass and there they would make milk.'

'I have brought you money,' I said. 'See, it is all green paper.'

But she looked at the paper unseeingly. I didn't like the look in her eyes. In the afternoon I took a walk round the graveyard near the house, and the tombstones were pink and engraved with names like conversation sweets.

There is nothing in the world worse than madness. All other diseases are trivial compared to it, for the light of reason is what illuminates the world. All that day I shouted to her, 'Come back to me', but she wouldn't. She wanted to stay in her cave of silence.

In this place I walk like a giant. My legs straddle the wardrobe, and the midgets around me speak with little mouths. My hands are too big for the table and my back for the chairs.

I look into the water which I brought home from the well and it is still and motionless. But my mother's eyes are slant and the old women whisper to her. I nearly chase them out of the house but my mother needs them, I think, for they tell old stories to each other. I think they are talking about the days when things were better than they are now.

The cat's mouth is wide open and he smiles all the time as if his mouth were fixed like that.

'Who are you?' says my mother, over and over. She doesn't remember the day she stood at the door watching me leave, a bag over my shoulder, her eyes shining with tears. I used to see her in the walls of skyscrapers, a transparency on stone. My young days were happy, I think, before she went crazy. Now and again she says things that I don't understand. She speaks the words, 'Who is the man with the black wings?' over and over. But when I ask her what she means she refuses to answer me.

Night falls, and there is a star like a silver coin in the sky. I hear the music of violins, and the black women have left. But my mother's eyes remain distant and hard, and she stares at me as if I were a stone. A dog with a plasticine body is barking from somewhere and in an attic a man is washing himself with soap over and over.

One day in New York I saw that the sun had a pair of moustaches like a soldier home from the wars, and he began to tell me a story.

'I went to the war,' he said, 'and I was eighteen years old. For no reason that I could think of, people began to fire at me trying to kill me. I stood by a tree that had red berries and prayed. I stayed there for a long time till the sun had gone down, counting the berries. After that I went home and I was hidden by my sister behind a large canvas for the rest of the war. When the war was over there were no trees to be seen.'

Still my mother stares at me with her unfocused eyes. I see the whites of them like the white of an egg. She has terrible dreams. In her dreams she is being chased by a vampire, and just at the moment when he is about to clutch her she wakens up.

'Where are you, my son?' she cries. I rush in, but she doesn't recognize me. The greatest gift in my life would be if she recognized me, if the light of reason would come back to her eyes.

I wonder now if it will ever happen.

'I shall put tap-water in the house for you,' I say to her. But she doesn't answer. She only picks at her embroidery.

'And heating,' I say. 'And an electric samovar.'

'My father,' she says, 'was a kind man who had a beard. He was often drunk but he would give you his last penny.'

I remember him. He wasn't kind at all. He was drunk and violent, and he had red eyes, and he played the violin all night. Sometimes I see him flying through the sky and his beard is a white cloud streaming behind him. But he was violent, gigantic and unpredictable.

Where the sky is greenest I can see him. I go to the cemetery with the pink tombstones, and his name isn't on any of them.

What am I to do with my mother, for she shouts at the policemen in the streets. 'Get out of here,' she screams at them, 'this was a road for cows in the old days.' The policemen smile and nod, and their tolerance is immense for she cannot harm them.

The bitterest tears I shed was when she told them that when her son came home he would show them that she wasn't to be treated like a tramp. The old, black women come back and are always whispering stories about her, but if I go near them they stop talking.

'Is your seed not growing yet?' I ask my next door neighbour.

'No,' he says, 'it is going to be a hard year. How is your mother?'

'Not well,' I say, 'she lives in a world of her own.'

He smiles, but says nothing. He was ten years old when I left this place with my bag on my shoulder. That day the birds were singing from the hedges and they each had one green eye and one blue.

I begin to draw my mother to see if her reason will come back to her. I see her as a path that has been overgrown with weeds. Her apron is a red phantom which one can hardly see and the chickens to which she threw meal have big ferocious beaks. Nevertheless, she does take an interest in what I am doing, though she cannot stay still, and her eyes are beginning to focus.

One day – the happiest of my life – she speaks to me again and recognizes me. 'You are my son,' she says, 'and you left me. Why did you leave me?' I try to tell her, but I cannot. The necessity for it is beyond her understanding, and this is the worst of all to bear.

That night before she goes to bed she says, 'Good night, my son,' and in the middle of the night she tucks the blanket about me to keep me warm. I feel that she is watching over me and I sleep better than I have done for many years. In the morning I am happy and wake up as the light pours through the windows. She is sitting by my bed with a shawl wrapped round her.

'Mother,' I cry, 'I am here. I have come back.' The windows change their shape as I say it. But she doesn't answer me. She is dead. She is a statue. She is solid and changeless. All that day I kneel in front of her, staring into her unchanging face.

In the evening one of her eyes becomes green and the other blue. I take my bag in my hand and leave the house. The birds are singing in the hedges and a man is walking through a ploughed field. I do not turn back and wave. The houses are turning into cardboard and the violins are stuck to their walls. I feel sticky stuff on my clothes, my hands and my face. I carry the village with me, stamped all over my body, and take it with me, roof, door, bird, branch, pails of water. I cross the Atlantic with it.

'Welcome,' they say, 'but what have you got there?'

'It is a nest,' I say, 'and a coffin.'

'Or, to put it another way, a coffin and a nest.'

Napoleon and I

I tell you what it is. I sit here night after night and he sits there night after night. In that chair opposite me. The two of us. I'm eighty years old and he's eighty-four. And that's what we do, we sit and think. I'll tell you what I sit and think about. I sit and think, I wish I had married someone else, that is what I think about.

And he thinks the same. I know he does. Though he doesn't say anything or at least much. Though I don't say much either. We have nothing to say: we have run out of conversation. That's what we've done. I look at his mouth and it's moving. But most of the time he's not speaking. I don't love him. I don't know what love is. I thought once I knew what love was. I thought it was something to do with being together for ever. I really thought that. Now I know that it's not that. At least it's not that, whatever else it is. *We do not speak to each other.*

He smokes a pipe sometimes and his mouth moves. He is like a cartoon. I used to read the papers and I used to see cartoons in them but now I don't read the papers at all. I don't read anything. Nor does he. Not even the sports pages though he once told me, no, more than once, he told me that he used to be a great footballer, 'When I used to go down the wing,' he would say. 'What wing?' I would say, and he would smile gently as if I were an idiot. 'When I used to go down the wing,' he would say. But now he doesn't go down any wing. He's even given up the tomato plants. And he imagines he's Napoleon. It's because of that film he says. There were red squares of soldiers in it. He sits in his chair as if he's Napoleon, and he says things to me in French though I don't know French and he doesn't know French. He prefers Napoleon to his tomato plants. He sits in his chair, his legs spread apart, and he thinks about winning Waterloo. I think he's mad. He must be, mustn't he? Sometimes he will look up and say 'Josephine', the one word 'Josephine', and the only work he ever did was in a distillery. Napoleon never worked in a distillery. I am sure that never happened. He's a comedian really. He sits there dreaming about Napoleon and sometimes he goes out and examines the ground to see if it's wet, if his cavalry will be all right. He kneels down and studies the ground and then he sits and puffs at his pipe and he goes and takes a pair of binoculars and he studies the landscape. I never thought he was Napoleon when I married him. I just said *I do*. Nor did he. I used to give him his sandwiches in a box when he went to work and he just took them in those days. I don't think he ever asked for wine. Now he thinks the world has mistreated him, and he wants an empire. Still they do say they need something when they retire. The only thing is, he's been retired for twenty years or maybe fifteen. He came home one day and he put his sandwich box on the table and he said, 'I'm retired' (that was in the days when we spoke to each other) and I said, 'I know that.' And he went and looked after his tomato plants. In those days he also loved the cat and was tender to his tomato plants. Now we no longer have a cat. We don't even have a tortoise. One day, the day he stopped speaking to me, he said, 'I've been hard done by. Life has done badly by me.' And he didn't say anything else. I think it was five o'clock on our clock that day, the 25th of March it would have been, or maybe the 26th.

Actually he looks stupid in that hat and that coat. Anyone would in the twentieth century.

I on the other hand spend most of my time making pictures with shells. I make a picture of a woman who has wings and who flies about in the sky and below her there is a man who looks like a prince and he is riding through a forest. The winged woman also has a cooker. I find it odd that she should have a cooker but there it is, why shouldn't she have a cooker if she wants to, I always say. On the TV everyone says, 'I always say', and then they have a cup of tea. At the most dramatic moments. And then I see him sitting opposite me in his Napoleon's coat and I think we are on TV. Sometimes I almost say that. But then I realize that we aren't speaking since we have nothing to speak about and I don't say anything. I don't even wash his coat for him.

In any case, how has he been hard done by? He married me, didn't he? I have given him the best years of my life. I have washed, scrubbed, cooked, slaved for him, and I have made sandwiches for him to put in his tin box every day. The same box.

And our children have gone away and they never came back. He used to say it was because of me, I say it's because of him. Who would want Napoleon for a father and anyway Napoleon didn't spend his time looking after tomato plants, though he doesn't do that now. He writes despatches which he gives to the milkman. He writes things like 'Tell Soult he must bring up another five divisions. Touty sweet.' And the milkman looks at the despatches and then he looks at me and then I give him the money for the week's milk. He is actually a very understanding milkman.

The fact that he wears a white coat is neither here nor there. Nothing is either here or there.

And sometimes he will have forgotten that the day before he asked for five divisions, and he broods, and he writes 'Please change the whole educational system of France. It is not just. And please get me a new sandwich box.'

He is really an unusual man. And I loved him once. I loved him when he was an ordinary man and when he would keep up an ordinary conversation when he would tell me what had happened at the distillery that day, though nothing much ever happened. Nothing serious. Nothing funny either. It was a very quiet distillery, and the whisky was made without trouble. Maybe it's because he left the distillery that he feels like

Napoleon. And he changed the chair too. He wanted a bigger
chair so that he could watch the army manoeuvres in the living-
room and yet have enough room for the TV-set and the fridge.
It's very hard living with a man who believes that there is an
army next to the fridge. But I think that's because he imagines
Napoleon in Russia, that's why he wants something cold.
And on days when Napoleon is in Russia he puts on extra
clothes and he wants plenty of meat in the fridge. The reason
for that I think is that the meat is supposed to be dead French
soldiers.

He is not mad really. He's just living in a dream. Maybe
he could have been Napoleon if he hadn't been born at 26
Sheffield Terrace. It's not easy being Napoleon if you're born
in a council house. The funny thing is that he never notices
the aerial. How could there be an aerial or even a TV-set in
Napoleon's time, but he doesn't notice that. Little things like
that escape him, though in other ways he's very shrewd. In
small ways. Like for instance he will remember and he'll say
to the milkman, 'You didn't bring me these five divisions
yesterday. Where the hell did you get to? Spain will kill me.'
And there will be a clank of bottles and the milkman will
walk away. That makes him really angry. Negligence of any
kind. Inefficiency. He'll get up and shout after him, 'How the
hell am I going to keep an empire together with idiots like
you about? EH? Tell me that, my fine friend.' Mr Merriman
thinks he is Joan of Arc. That causes a lot of difficulty with
dresses though not as much as you would imagine since she
wore men's armour anyway. I dread the day Wellington will
move in. I fear for my china.

Anyway that's why we don't speak. Sometimes he doesn't
even recognize me and he calls me Antoinette and he throws
things at me. I don't know what to do, really I don't. I'm at
my wits' end. It would be cruel to send for a doctor. I don't
hate him that much. I think maybe I should tell him I'm leaving
but where can you go when you're eighty years old, though
he is four years younger than me; I would have to get a home
help: he doesn't think of things like that. One day he said to

me, 'I don't need you. I don't need anyone. My star is here.'
And he pointed at his old woollen jacket which had a large
hole in it. Sometimes I can hardly keep myself from laughing
when I'm doing my shells. Who could? Unless one was an
angel?

And then sometimes I think, Maybe he's trying it on. And
I watch out to see if I can trap him in anything, but I haven't
yet. His despatches are very orderly. He sends me orders like,
'I want the steak underdone today. And the wine at a moderate
temperature.' And I make the beefburgers and coffee as usual.

Yesterday he suddenly said, 'I remember you. I used to
know you, when we were young. There were woods. I
associate you with woods. With autumn woods.' And then
his face became slightly blue. I thought he was going to fall,
coming out of his dream. But no. He said, 'It was outside
Paris and I met you in a room with mirrors. I loved you once
before my destiny became my sorrow.' These were exactly
his words, I think. He never used to talk like that. He would
mostly grunt and say, 'What happened to the salt?' But now
he doesn't say anything as simple as that. No indeed. Not at all.

Sometimes he draws up a chair and dictates notes to me.
He says things like, 'We attack the distillery at dawn. Junot
will create a diversion on the left and then Soult will strike at
the right while I punch through the centre.'

He was never in a war in his life. He was kept out because
of his asthma and his ulcer. And he never had a horse in his
life. All he had was his sandwich box. And now he wants a
coronet on it. Imagine, a coronet on a sandwich box. Will this
never end? Ever? Will it? I suffer. It is I who put up with this
for he never leaves the house, he is too busy organizing the
French educational service and the Church. 'We will have pink
robes for the nuns,' he says. 'That will teach them the power
of the flesh which they *abominate*,' and he shouts across the
fence at Joan of Arc and says, 'You're an impostor, sir. Joan
of Arc didn't have a moustache.' I don't know what I shall
do. He is sitting there so calm now, so calm with his stick in
his hand like a sceptre. I think he has fallen asleep. Let me put

your crown right, child. It's fallen all to one side. I could never stand untidiness. Let me pick up your stick, its fallen from your hand. We are doomed to be together. We are doomed to say to the milkman, 'Bring up your five divisions', for morning after morning. We are doomed to comment on Joan of Arc's moustache. We are together for ever. Poor Napoleon. Poor lover of mine met long ago in the autumn woods before they became your empire. Poor dreamer.

And yet... what a game... maybe I should try on your crown just for one moment, just for a short moment. And take your stick just for a moment, just for a short short moment. Before you wake up. And maybe I'll tell the milkman, We want ten divisions today. Ten not five. Maybe that would be the best idea, to get it finished with, once and for all. Ten instead of five.

And don't forget the cannon.

Christmas Day

ON that Christmas Day she was the only customer in the hotel for lunch. 'I shall take the turkey soup,' she said. The dining-room was very large and she sat at her table as if she was on a desert island. Above her head were green streamers and green hats and in the middle of the dining-room there was a green tree.

Somewhere in Asia the peasants were digging.

'The fact is,' she thought, 'I'll never see him again. He is irretrievably dead.' The pain was inside her like a jagged star.

There was this particular peasant with a bald head and when he was finished digging he went home to his family and played the guitar. It might have been China or Korea but when his mouth moved she didn't understand what he was saying. To think, she mused, that there were all these peasants in the world, and all these languages.

She drank her turkey soup and watched the two waitresses talking, their arms folded.

She had watched him die for three weeks. His pain was intolerable. After that there were the papers to be checked. One day she had left the house with a case and gone to the hotel in which she now was.

There were millions of peasants in the world and millions of paddy fields, and they all sang strange unintelligible songs. Some of them rode on bicycles through Hong Kong.

'I love you,' he had said at the end. Their hands had tightened on eternity. When she withdrew her hand the pulse was beating but his had stopped.

She wished to change her chair so that she could not see the waitresses, but she was naked and throbbing to their gaze.

When she had entered her room in the hotel for the first time she had switched on the television-set. It showed peasants working in the fields in the East. She had picked up the phone and wondered whom she could talk to. Perhaps to one of the peasants in their wide-brimmed hats. She had put the phone down.

There were twenty of them in the one house, children, parents, grandparents, aunts and uncles and they were all smiling as if their paddy fields generated light.

'I am thin as a pencil,' she thought. 'Why did I wear this grey costume and this necklace?'

She finished the turkey soup. Then she tried to eat the turkey. For me it was killed, with its red comb, its splendid feathers, its small unperplexed head on the long and reptilian neck. Nevertheless I must eat.

Wherever Tom had gone, he had gone. 'Put me in a glass box,' he used to say. 'I want people to make sure that I am dead.' But in fact he had been cremated. She heard that the coffins swelled out with the heat, but he had laughed when she had told him. 'Put me in an ashtray in the living-room.'

The smoke rose above the paddy fields and the peasants were crouched around it.

She left much of the turkey and then took ice cream which was cold in her mouth. She was alone in the vast dining-room.

Christmas was the loneliest time of all. No one who had not experienced it could believe how lonely Christmas could be, how conspicuous the unaccompanied were.

From the paddy field the peasant raised his face smiling and it was Tom's face.

'Hi,' he said in a fluting Korean voice.

The green paper hats above her swayed slightly in the draught which rippled the carpet below. It seemed quite natural that he should be sitting in front of her in his wide-brimmed hat.

'The heat wasn't at all unbearable,' he said.

He took out a cracker and pulled it. He read out what was written on the little piece of paper. It said, 'Destiny waits for us like a bus.' Or a rickshaw.

The world was big and it pulsed with life. Dinosaurs walked about like green ladders and bowed gently to the ants who were carrying their burdens. The peasant sat in a ditch and played his guitar and winked at her.

'I remember,' said Tom scratching his neck, 'someone once saying that the world appears yellow to a canary. Even sorrow, even grief.'

And red to a turkey.

She got up and went to her room walking very straight and stiff so that the waitresses' glances would bounce off her back. Who wanted pity when death was so common?

She sat on her bed and picked up the phone.

She dialled her own number and heard the phone ringing in an empty house.

'If only he would answer it,' she said. 'If only he would answer it.'

Then she heard the voice. It said, 'Who is that speaking, please.'

She knew it was Tom and that he was wearing a wide-brimmed hat.

'I shall be home soon,' she said.

She took off her clothes and went to bed. When she woke up she felt absolutely refreshed and her head was perfectly clear.

She packed up her case, paid her bill at the desk and went home.

When she went in she heard the guitar being played upstairs. She knew that they would all be there, all the happy peasants, and sitting among them, quite at home, Tom in his green paper hat with the wine bottle in his hand.

The Arena

IT was at Pula that she had the vision that she would never forget. She had taken Paul there on the bus and he was rather tired as usual. Ever since his big operation he had been tired and at the end of their holiday he was going back to another operation. According to himself his boss had been rather kind and had said, picking up the phone that lay in front of him on the desk, 'Paul has been with us for thirty years. There is no question of this half-pay nonsense.' Paul worked as a clerk in the Civil Service and had never missed a day till his operation. He had been in severe pain for a while and no one knew what was wrong with him till the specialist had finally diagnosed it as an aortic aneurism. He had lost a lot of weight and looked thin and drawn.

When she looked back over the years she realized that their life together had been on the whole a peaceful one. But she wondered if in fact the disease had come because Paul was tired of his work though he used to tell her, 'When I first started I was happy. I can't tell you how happy I was. And then it all changed. We used to have a joke together in those days but now it's all different.'

He had many little anecdotes to tell her, such as the one about the day when quite young he had been doing an imitation of the manager, an imaginary pipe stuck in his mouth when the latter had put his head round the door and caught him. 'He was a man entirely without humour,' he said. 'And after that I beat him at billiards.'

But of course that had been a different manager from the

one they now had. 'Another time,' he said, 'he made an awful speech on the retiral of a lady member of staff and I was the only one who clapped. He stared at me, I remember, as if he couldn't make up his mind whether I was laughing at him or not. His speeches were terrible.'

According to himself he had been a ball of fire in those days, fiery with wit and inventiveness. And he had told her the same stories over and over so much that she sometimes wondered whether her boredom was becoming unbearable. Still he had taken his illness with admirable stoicism, not complaining much, accepting his destiny with dignity.

But in a country like this one saw only the healthy ones, especially in summer and they all looked so beautiful and tanned beside Paul.

They bloomed with luminous health, they seemed to have the sheen of animals: while all the time the sun was a fierce bristly animal in a sky of unchanging blue.

As well as being a civil servant, Paul also umpired cricket matches on Sundays and she knew that he missed the cool green misty afternoons when in his white surgical coat he would stand there making decisions. He himself believed that umpiring was his real vocation: it certainly gave him more scope for decision-making than the Civil Service did.

A youth walked along in front of her. He looked dark and Italian and had the most beautiful arrogant buttocks. How self-confident he was, how extraordinarily alive and lovely. At that very moment she would have gone with him to a dance, a gipsy dance, to drink wine, to make love. She couldn't imagine him in the Civil Service sitting down at a desk day after day, picking up a phone and saying to a caller who perhaps had an upper-class accent:

'I'm sorry, sir, but we don't keep a record of that,' and the man with the upper-class accent saying contemptuously:

'But aren't you a clerk or something? Shouldn't you know that sort of thing?'

No, that youth would never be servile or slavish, he would never reach that stage in his life when he would become so depressingly proud and say, 'And Spence took up the phone and said, No damn nonsense about half-pay. Mason's been with us for thirty years.'

She could imagine Paul leaning forward obediently, subserviently, the manager swivelling arrogantly in his chair in a careless arc as if he were on a machine at a fairground.

So many of these youths, so beautiful, so young, and herself growing old, and into her menopause. She dragged Paul along like a chain behind her: he clanked in the hot day of her mind.

Conscience-stricken that she had almost thought of him like a slave she pointed out a wallet to him in a window that they were passing and asked him if he wanted it but he didn't, he considered it too cheap and tawdry. He seemed to evaluate it with agonizing slowness as if deciding whether it was like a cricketer who should be given out.

Finally, he said, 'It's not worth the money.' He was very good at converting lire and dinars into English money, far quicker than she was. But these days there was a faraway look in his eyes as if he was staring at the green ring of a damp cricket field.

No, he had never been a flashing batsman or a demon bowler, only a very calm considering umpire, one who was weighty and careful in his decisions: and perhaps he would never be an umpire again. Perhaps he would never stand in his white coat under an amateur sky.

Her body boiled with the heat and, she was ashamed to admit, desire. The two of them hadn't had sex for the last three months. Funny expression that, 'had sex' or 'made love' when what she really meant was what she imagined these foreigners as doing, devouring each other's bodies in the sun. Images of bodies clawed and mated and fought in her mind. They leaped ravenously out of dark secret corners into the arena of her sunlight. They were strong and powerful and had nothing at all to do with the calm fields over which her husband had presided in the intervals of his dedicated work for the Civil Service.

'Are you all right?' said Paul curiously. 'You seem to be sweating a lot.'

'It's very hot,' she said.

Her body seethed with the heat, she almost fainted with the savagery of the images that leaped about in her mind, no, not in her mind, in the secret caverns and hollows of her body. And she was ashamed of them as Paul slowly paced beside her.

No, she must confront the question: what would she do if Paul died? Would she marry again? Could she bear to be alone? She had never been alone in her life, she had come from a large noisy family, animated with anecdote and discussion, and she didn't really know what solitude was. Also, she had never been a reader, she had always been happier with physical things, the confused chatter of kids in the school canteen where she served. But the question nevertheless had to be faced. When they returned to England and he had his operation he might die and what would she do then? Could she stay alone in the house after the day's work was over, could she watch television endlessly? Not that she had anyone in mind to replace Paul, nor had she ever been intimate with anyone but him. She smiled to herself at the archaic oddity of the expression.

Could she perhaps fling up her job and do what she had always wanted to do, that is wander about like a gipsy? But that would be impossible, an idle dream. Even gipsies didn't live on air, they too needed food, drink, a bed. No she couldn't leave the little terraced house bought with Paul's blood and the garden which he kept so tidy. Nor could she abandon her job. Paul wouldn't have much money to leave, though he had now stopped drinking and smoking.

Did she love him? Did she truly love him? The question struck at her like a blow from the sun. She thought she loved him and was sure that he loved her. But what was real love like? Had she ever truly experienced it? Was love involved with sex? Could she love someone without having sex with them?

It was odd how grey his hair was becoming, she hadn't noticed the greyness so clearly before. And how dependent he was growing on her, he who had always planned the details of their holidays so meticulously, taking a pride in doing so. She did not like his new passiveness: it was significant and ominous. In the past he used to love working out itineraries, even keeping a diary. And now he had given all that up. It was as if he was sensing an eternity which had no need of notes.

And another thing, he never told her what happened in the office. In the old days he used to bring home a hoard of stories like the one for instance about the tramp who used to come to the office to collect his social security and say, 'You think I'm going to die and save you money but I'm not.' And he would glare fiercely around him, unshaven, gaunt, indomitable. She could imagine him, obstinate in his determination to stay alive.

Or he might tell her about Miss Collins and Mr White who hadn't spoken to each other for years because Miss Collins had arranged the chairs for a meeting without telling him about it beforehand.

Oh God, this tremendous heat, this desire, this unfocused lust. Did others suffer from this? Did others appear to walk calmly along while raging inwardly like beasts within their pale pelts? And why was she feeling that desire now, was it the heat that was causing it, or the threat of death, or was it that she was simply ageing?

'Are you feeling all right?' she asked. She was always asking the same question as if out of a sense of profound guilt that followed both of them like shadows. Paul was sweating, not her brimming natural sweat but a grey chilly sweat. Her sweat on the other hand was the bloom on the fruit about to burst, before it hangs and shrivels like a rag on a tree.

When Paul wore his umpire's coat he looked like a doctor or a waiter. Not that she had seen him umpiring for many years. He stood there in the green light and a man would be out – his wickets sent flying – or a catch would be granted. As an umpire, Paul had a certain power. But she didn't like cricket, it was very slow, it was so slow that it felt like an eternity happening in front of her eyes. All you could hear was sporadic clapping as if from a grave and then silence.

But that didn't disguise the question she had to face. Did she love Paul? And the most tremendous question of all was, would she be glad when he died? Would she be glad when she heard no more about the Civil Service or cricket? Would she be glad when she was no longer in the presence of his greyness?

'There it is,' said Paul suddenly.

'What?' she asked as if emerging from a dream.

'The amphitheatre,' he said.

And she saw it then, a big circular stone building with rows of arches and window spaces.

'Do you want to go in?' he asked.

Seeing that he was tired she was not sure what she should say, but he added, 'I think we should see it. It's the only worthwhile thing in Pula.'

Of course he would have read about it, of course he would know its history. If he had nothing else he had information.

As they paid and entered, the heat was appalling.

'Do you know the story about it?' Paul asked. 'Why it doesn't have a roof?'

'No,' she said.

His gaunt face softened. 'It's a charming story. It is said that fairies built the amphitheatre with big stones they carted from all over Istria. They began building it at night. However at cockcrow the fairies ran away and left the building without a roof on it.'

'How beautiful,' she said. In her mind's eye she saw bronze cocks crowing, pulsing throats outstretched, wings clapping. Paul had become animated for a moment: he was like a pupil showing off to a teacher. The cocks crew and the fairies flew away and there was no roof on the amphitheatre. The fairies like gipsies departed in the night, in their irresponsible glamour. If it had been Paul he would definitely have completed the roof, for he always finished what he began.

The stone around her was intensely hot. In front of her she saw the young men and women from all over Asia and Europe with their vibrant fragrant impudent bodies. The throbbing heat pulsed from the stone, from her body.

'Listen,' said Paul, 'to the right and left there were areas where wild animals were kept. They were released into the arena.'

'Did they fight each other?'

'They fought with the gladiators and the slaves. The front seats in the gallery were reserved for the important people, the patricians. There used to be a lot of women spectators. Some of them were the worst.'

'The worst?' she said.

'The most cruel.'

And the Civil Servants, she thought, where were they? And the cool umpires? She had a dim memory that there used to be someone important who raised or lowered his thumb, as the gladiator turned and looked up into the blinding sunlight, foreshortened, waiting for his doom to be signalled, his fortune to be told.

And at that moment she felt a storm of sound around her. The arena was a writhing medley of legs, arms, torsos, swords: the lithe lions eeled forward like cats stalking birds. Then they leaped in an arc of claws and teeth. She saw a gladiator on the ground and another one standing above him, his legs spread wide in an arrogant posture.

The one on the ground was Paul and his face was throbbing in the sun, especially a big blue vein in his forehead, and there were rays of blood across his cheek. The other one – but who was the other one? She couldn't see his face but his private parts were massive, his penis throbbed like a hammer between the two big bells, the colour of flesh. Far away was the green field and the cloudy sky. There was a man in a white uniform in the middle of the arena turning his thumb down over Paul. There was a chaos of gnawing beasts, jaws, teeth, and in the centre of it all a cockerel crowing. Her whole body throbbed with fire: she was a womb that burned and flamed. Her eyes were blind and hollow and made of stone, as she turned them on Paul. She was an empress, a sleek lioness. Somewhere in a stony room underground a man was scribbling furiously

with a stony pen forever and forever, his brow wrinkled as if
with puzzlement. He was bent over, keeping records of all
the animals, he was making sure that the timetable of furious
deaths was adhered to. Then she saw him rising slowly and
ascending into the arena. A lioness, tawny and almost loving,
was waiting for him. She sniffed and her eyes were golden
and lazy and calm. Her mane was like a circlet of fire around
her. She trotted towards him easily and he waited there quite
tranquilly, his hands loose at his sides. He was scrutinizing
the lioness silently as if asking her a question.

Do you want me? Do you love me?

And the lioness trotted towards him. The empress was
standing up. In a short while she would turn her thumb down
or up. The crowd was roaring, itself like a wild beast, and
the sun was a torrent of fire.

The man was looking into the eyes of the lioness. He was
wearing a white coat, he was standing in the middle of the
stone field.

Her loins shuddered and dampened.

Paul was leaning out of the sun and was saying to her, 'Are
you all right? Are you frightened or something?'

She felt the tears streaming down her face.

'What's the matter?' he was saying over and over in a concerned voice. The lioness had shrunk back to its den. The
fairies had flown away. The cockerel had started flapping its
wings.

'Come on,' she said, 'let's go.'

It was too late. It was not a question of loving or being
loved. The last blood had been and gone. This had been a
country of the sun, merciless and hot, and she had missed it.
In this country one didn't ask about love, one either loved or
one didn't. The ring of stone which encircled her wasn't hers.

If you had been umpire here, she nearly said to him, if you
had been umpire here what would you have done? This was
no amateurish play on a Sunday, this had been an affair of life
and death, of real claws, real teeth.

She looked down at her damp green dress, and nearly wept

with the pity of it. She would stay with him till morning, till the roof of stone went on. She would not leave at cockcrow or in the middle of the night. She would not fly away on negligent wings.

The apples that moved ahead of her, these round buttocks were distant and belonged to another country. She dare not touch them, not in this ring of stone, in this arena from which the blood had departed.

The Tour

DAPHNE hadn't thought that she would enjoy herself so much, though at first she had been rather stiff and formal, finding it difficult to break the shell of her English private school up-bringing, which had been followed by her marriage to Geoffrey, a captain in the British Army who was now in Australia, posted there for a year. But as the bus tour progressed she found that it was impossible to keep herself apart from the rest of the passengers, however she might try to do so. And it really wasn't arrogance that was the armour that stood between her and the others, not at all, it was, she knew, her accent that separated them and made them suspicious of her. Her martial stiffness was odd and imperial and very British and they resented it in their inner being.

Yet it was odd how, unlike Geoffrey, she had liked Australia from the beginning, though it was in its dusty acreages so different from the green fields of England. She belonged, she thought, with a wry smile, to the world of that school in the film *Picnic at Hanging Rock* with its iron grey mistresses.

Geoffrey didn't like Australia, he thought of it as a country of beer-swilling yobs, of undisciplined soldiers. He had once related to her a story of what had happened during the war to an officer much older than himself, who had told him of it.

'He was standing at this railway station,' he said, 'waiting for a train, and he saw this mob of Australian soldiers walking up and down. None of them saluted him. So he gave them a bollocking. And do you know what they did? They marched up and down for the rest of the time, very stiff and proper, saluting him every time they passed him.'

She had tried not to laugh but she couldn't help it.

'What the hell are you laughing at?' Geoffrey had said in his stiff upright manner.

'Nothing, nothing,' she had replied between giggles. 'Nothing at all.' And Geoffrey had fumed at her, angry as if she were a green silly schoolgirl.

But she loved Australia. She loved its mystery, she imagined it as a childish book illustrated with pictures of dingoes, kookaburras, emus. The centre of it was an echo that wished to become a voice, that wished to say, 'I am me.' It had no ranks, no orders, it was an efflorescence of wild spiky flowers, and lonely marvellous deserts.

It was the retired schoolmistress whom she liked best of all. Whenever the bus stopped at a hotel she was the first to rush to the gambling machines – the one-armed bandits – that were to be found everywhere: and with the curious careless innocence of a seventy-year-old who no longer cared for convention, she would plunge her hand in among a cascade of coins. Her name was Casey and she belonged originally to Sydney where she had taught for forty years.

'Didn't you know that we Australians are a nation of gamblers?' she said to Daphne. 'Everywhere you go there are these machines.' Her hair was cropped and grey and she moved with great rapidity and animation like a little very positive animal.

'No, I didn't know,' said Daphne. Neither she nor Geoffrey had gambled in their lives. She knew that in any battle, if there was a battle, he would prepare for every contingency, he wouldn't make a move without checking and cross checking; she thought of him as a machine in a tight uniform, like one of those early redcoats.

And so she watched Miss Casey, who had never married, plunging her hands among the coins as if she were a virgin immersing herself in a waterfall in a land that was brilliant with sunshine.

'Luck is everything,' said Miss Casey, 'I have been lucky

all my life. I loved my children,' as she called her pupils, 'and now I am enjoying myself. What is the point of not?' And she gazed at Daphne with a bland guileless eye, the eye of one who has transcended it with inward bubbling joy. She was the first to get up in the morning and was to be found exploring among the woods and the dew.

At first the hare-lipped Miss Cowan didn't speak to them at all. She sat by herself in the bus, staring out of the window, clutching her handbag. When she did at last speak it was on their tour of the wineries when they were all tasting different wines.

'You could spend all your days doing this,' said Miss Casey delightedly. 'I'm sure there must be some people who do it.' She sipped appreciatively. 'What do you think of this one?' she asked Miss Cowan, and Miss Cowan in words that one could hardly understand because of her harelip, answered, 'It's sweet.'

As a matter of fact Daphne disliked deformity of any kind; but that had been a hilarious day, seven wineries in one day, and the driver had smiled when they had asked him, 'Are you sure you can drive after all this?' Imagine it though, seven wineries in one day, it wasn't the sort of thing that Geoffrey would have approved of. Bad organization he would have said, surely they could have organized the trip better than that! A whole day wasted at wineries! But even Miss Cowan blossomed and was in fact slightly tipsy on that blue marvellous day, and Miss Casey had been very animated.

Daphne enjoyed herself immensely though she was sorry for Miss Cowan. To think that she could hardly be understood by anyone! No wonder she kept silent, no wonder she withdrew from them all. It must be awful to try and speak and come out with these awful strangulated sounds.

Eventually there were five of them that went about together, herself, Miss Casey, Miss Cowan, and that ex-policeman from Glasgow, Mr Wilson, and his wife. He was a squat energetic interesting man who had served so he had said in Borneo before coming to Australia; his wife was quiet, slim, fair-haired. He was determined to enjoy his trip.

And so they sailed on the Murray River, and had a look in
the museum at Echuca where Prince Philip in upright glassy
splendour was to be seen among more macabre exhibits.
Echuca was slummier than she had expected, the rag-end of
a once prosperous town, though the paddle steamers were
quaint and romantic and ponderous.

'Did you hear this one?' said Mr Wilson. 'There were these
two Glasgow football supporters and they went to Italy and
they went into a pub and one of them said,

"What do you sell here?"

And the barman said, "Chianti."

"Whit's that?" said one of them. "We'll take a pint."

And they took a pint each and they got very drunk and as
they were staggering along one of them said to the other,

"No wonder they carry the Pope about in a chair."'

They had all laughed, Miss Casey in short concentrated
bursts like machine gun fire, Daphne more decorously. Then
she felt constrained to tell some of her own stories, for she
felt that the Wilsons weren't sure of her, thought of her as a
Southern English type.

She felt awkward beginning her story. 'It was one day,' she
said, and then casually, 'My husband Geoff is an officer. And
this general's wife came to visit us. This was in Australia. I
had tried to talk to her, usual stuff I thought you should talk
about to generals' wives, and she sat there, a big woman, and
then after a while she got up and said,

"See you later."

And I thought,' she began to laugh, 'and I thought she was
going to come back that same day. And when Geoff came
home I was in a panic. I told him that I had gone out to buy
a new dress because I didn't want the general's wife to see me
in the same dress twice in the one day. And Geoff said,

"Don't you know that saying,

'See you later' is like saying

'Cheerio.'"

But I had actually gone out to buy a new dress. Actually.'
And Miss Casey laughed and said,

'Of course you were not expected to know that.' She herself went on to cap the story with another one.

'There was this friend of mine who was staying in London. And she caught a cold and stayed in bed. A friend of hers, English, phoned her up and asked her to come and visit her. No, she said, I can't, I'm in bed with a wog. You see "wog" in Australia means a "germ".'

They had all dissolved in hysterical laughter though it seemed to Daphne that some of the others had heard the story before. Miss Cowan making odd guttural noises, her moustache trembling at her lip.

'What she must have thought,' said Daphne, 'what she must have thought.' And she saw this proper woman in bed in a London hotel with a wog stretched at her side. 'Wog' was the very word that Geoffrey might have used about the Australians.

The bus crossed the border into Victoria which was much greener than the area from which they had come. It looked exactly like England, with its green fertile land; she could imagine a private school set here among the fruit trees.

And then there was the day they stopped at the Chinese cemetery. There was Chinese writing on the tombstones, indecipherable among the wild grass.

Miss Casey gazed at the cemetery in amazement. 'It's like seeing restaurants,' she said. 'Restaurants of dead people.' And Tom Wilson shouted, 'Made in Hong Kong,' while his wife looked on disapprovingly. Daphne thought Mrs Wilson didn't like her, fearing that Tom might get off with her, for she was young and girlish and upper class. Daphne didn't think that the Wilsons were well off though Tom was incredibly generous, insisting on paying for the drinks whenever they stopped at a hotel.

They wandered through the graveyard, Daphne saying to Miss Cowan, 'They don't look after their graveyards very well here, do they' (thinking of the ranked stone doors of English graveyards), and Miss Cowan made her usual strangulated noises, like a radio not quite tuned to a station, and

Daphne thought she heard her say that Australians moved on a great deal, wouldn't stay long in one place.

'I will tell you what happened here,' said Miss Casey, as if she were teaching the class from the centre of the overgrown graveyard. 'There was a lot of Chinese labour here at one time, and it was treated abominably. That is why this grave-yard is so large. Look,' she said, 'this is where they made their offerings to the dead.' Miss Cowan in her dumb way bent down to interrogate the indecipherable language on the stones. Daphne briefly remembered her walk through the Chinese quarter of Vancouver and the Chinese signs on the telephone kiosks.

They stood silently in the graveyard among the wild over-grown grass, the sun hot on their heads like a burning helmet in the sky. We are all gathered here, thought Daphne, me from my leafy school, the Wilsons from Glasgow, Miss Casey the schoolmistress from Sydney, and Miss Cowan from I don't know where. All I know about her is that she has an invalid sister and that she goes on a bus trip once a year, with her harelip and her moustache.

And the sky was blue above them, and there were some brightly coloured birds flying from branch to branch, and the signs on the stones were inscrutably Chinese. The poor labour-ing foreigners came to this land, toiled and died, and were buried in a country which did not know enough to interpret their epitaphs. The Chinese had died indecipherably among the stones.

It was in silence that they went back to the bus but the silence didn't last long for Tom Wilson began to imitate their driver who also acted as their guide.

'And there straight ahead of us is Bare Hill,' he said. 'It is called Bare Hill because there is nothing on top of it. Once there was a winery but it fell into disuse over the years. On your left you can see Goat Hill because it was once inhabited by goats. You will notice that it has the shape of a big cheese.' And they all thought the commentary hysterically funny, Tom imitated the driver so well, he was so jolly, he drew new ideas and sights out of the air around him, out of this Australia which she was beginning to love so much. And already she had forgotten about the Chinese labourers and the cemetery. O how young she felt, how happy, how glad she had come: she felt so diaphanous and clean and leafy. And she could have waved a hand to make Miss Cowan speak. But Miss Cowan couldn't speak properly, you had to listen very patiently to her to understand her, it was as if she was trying continually to move a step up the evolutionary scale, like those animals and birds halted in their upward drive, these freaks, these speechless beings.

And on a night with a hard metallic moon in the sky like a yellow medal they played one-up with coins in a Club after the Anzac Day military parade. And Miss Casey played the gambling machines and won. So that back in the hotel that night, after they had seen the aged veterans marching, they had not wanted to go to bed. And miracle of miracles they had found a piano in the big hotel dining-room and Tom had bought them schooners of beer, and Miss Cowan had played for them. Such talent too! Who could have foreseen that Miss Cowan would be such a pianist. But she had been, and she had known all the songs, and Tom had sung 'Loch Lomond', while pretending he was wearing a kilt and in that Australian world with its images of Gallipoli they had listened to him singing of his country with sweetness and power. Then Daphne had been asked to sing and she couldn't bring herself to do so, with all her English reticence, that final barrier which she hadn't broken. Even Mrs Wilson, though reluctantly, had sung, though she herself hadn't dared to. Once she thought of singing 'Greensleeves' but considered it somehow unsuitable. She regretted that very much. But Miss Casey had flung her skirt about and had sung 'Waltzing Matilda' and finally they had a huge concert going in that big bare dining-room whose seats had been cleared to the sides, with Anzac veterans there, and Miss Cowan had tirelessly played the piano, and had been kissed by a large Australian with a fat belly and a lot of medals on his chest. Miss Cowan was really glowing, not having to speak at all, the centre of attention, a queen whose harelip had been forgotten. It was like a fairy story.

And so they had gone to bed very late and she had been restless and had stood at the window and seen through it a moon like a shrunken aboriginal bone, shining in the sky. And she had undressed and stood there white and pearly, thinking of green England, with Geoffrey standing at attention on a green field and herself about to play hockey, watched by a schoolmistress with short grey hair who was blowing a whistle for the game to begin. O Lord how beautiful this is, she thought, these lovely Scottish songs, these high roads and low roads, these ghostly soldiers, as Tom had explained them. And she was angry with herself because she hadn't sung 'Greensleeves' as she had intended to, for after all it was a beautiful song too. Her not singing it had been a betrayal!

And the moon hung there like a curved bone, ancient, aboriginal, the bone from which the world had been made, as if it were a continual interrogation, but really speechless and blank, the shape of Miss Cowan's mouth, but with no harelip on it. Miss Cowan who had played the piano so well; Daphne could play the piano too, and had been taught to do so, though she had left Miss Cowan to her triumph that night in her speechless glow. And somewhere not far away the Wilsons were sleeping and Geoffrey too was sleeping in his cold military bed and Miss Casey was dreaming of her pupils.

In the morning she was up bright and early and waiting for the bus. She felt a constraint in the atmosphere as if the Wilsons had been quarrelling during the night, as if Mrs Wilson had been saying to Tom, 'I don't like the way you talk so much to the snooty Daphne. Don't you realize that you are making a fool of yourself? She doesn't belong to our class. She is only amusing herself. And she wouldn't even sing, pretending that she didn't know the words.'

And in this atmosphere of constraint the bus made its way towards Beechworth, Ned Kelly country. From the bag in which she kept the koala bear she had bought for Shirley, her little daughter, she took the reproductions by Nolan and studied

them while Mrs Wilson stared out of the window and Tom
was unusually silent, a bearlike hulk which had been stood in
a corner. How funny these paintings were, Ned Kelly with
his box-like mask peering from between slim green tree
trunks. And the funniest of all was the policeman, head down
in a hole, only his legs, straight and blue, to be seen, while a
quizzical bird perched on a precarious branch looking at him.
The box-like mask was like a television-set. The butt of a rifle
stuck in the ground had fingers at the end of it. Funny old
surrealistic paintings. And Ned Kelly, the bandit, the anarchic
chaotic Irishman, the one whom Geoffrey would have hunted
down remorselessly, if he had been living at the time, Geoffrey
like that policeman upside down in the hole, still so correct
in his blue uniform. And perhaps Miss Casey herself had Irish
ancestry with her love of gambling, her uncaring innocence,
Miss Casey who had loved her pupils all her childlike life.

And Beechworth when they arrived at it was like an Old
Wild West frontier town. And they saw the Rock Cavern with
its glittering gems and minerals, a fairyland of colour. And
the gold vault where the dummy with white shirt and black
waistcoat weighed gold on a scales while behind him there
was a green safe. Oh, it was really like another world, a world
now of order which had once been anarchic. Why had it all
disappeared? Why had the men in tight blue cloth destroyed
the green anarchic Irishry?

And they had wandered through the museum looking at
the Ned Kelly stuff, the frail looking armour and guns. Why
had she thought the armour would be more solid than it was?
But imagine a man thinking of that, wearing armour. It took
Irish imagination to think of that. It was so medieval and
romantic among these spiky flowers so far from Westminster
Abbey, and for that matter from Buckingham Palace in which
bright aluminium-coloured armour still concealed Her
Majesty's soldiers. But the frail armour of Ned Kelly was like
a holed leaf with the rot of autumn in it. That frail armour,
those horses, in the middle of Australia so long ago. So that
she had stood beside Miss Cowan who was looking at the

armour, the mask, with a strange longing, and suddenly quite out of the blue she had been startled by the thought,

That is what she wants, that armour. She has taught no pupils as Miss Casey has done, she has never married like Mrs Wilson and me, she doesn't have the armour to protect and conceal herself from the world. She wants to be secretive and hidden like myself long ago in those leafy woods round my private school, in my green leafy uniform and speaking my Latin; like Tom Wilson behind the sweetness of 'Loch Lomond'. Perhaps Tom doesn't like being in Australia, she thought, perhaps he really wants to go home, perhaps he will have to stay here forever, perhaps too his wife hates being here, for she often talks about her mother on some council estate in Glasgow, dying there, not to be seen again, among these stones with the indecipherable writing on them; perhaps she wants to be home with her, before she is laid to rest in that stony windy jungle. We are all exiles, frightened of the world. But she wasn't frightened of the world, she loved Australia, she loved its wildness, its strangeness, its unranked foliage. And she loved Geoffrey too though sometimes she couldn't stand his correctness and stiffness, she thought him comic in his uprightness, in his meticulousness, she saw him upside down in the hole, in his tight uniform while the mocking TV box stared at him from behind a tall green tree trunk, and the military abrasive kookaburra glared at him like the general's wife. And she thought of the emu she had seen in the zoo to which the driver had taken them and which was an albino and had to be kept apart from the other emus for they would have killed it because of its strangeness, like Miss Cowan, the separate one, the one who did not belong. And at that moment she touched Miss Cowan lightly as the latter stared at the mask and it was as if something in her own breast, her womb, overflowed, as if it were water, tears.

And they walked back in silence to the bus through the calm serene air of Beechworth, the Wilsons still not speaking to each other, Miss Casey lost in a dream of her own.

Oh, except that she did buy a towel for Miss Cowan on

which were written the words of 'Amazing Grace' and Miss Cowan's gratitude was so excessive that she felt ashamed. To be going on bus trips year after year in order to rest for a while from the demands made on her by her invalid sister, but at least taking back with her this time memories of her hours at the piano, of Tom Wilson's horseplay, of the funny commentary, of the wineries, of the sail on Murray River, of the towel with its religious words, a gift freely given. The possible grace of speech that Miss Cowan took away from her enchanted stare at the mask set in the middle of the tamed town!

And that was the high part of the tour, that visit to the once wild land where Ned Kelly and his Irishry had taken on the establishment. The road unspooled through the evening: it was as if they all really wanted to go home now, exchanging addresses at the back of the bus. 'You must visit us,' said Daphne to her four friends, though she wasn't sure whether they would or not, whether they thought she really meant the invitation seriously. Rank was closing in on them like the evening. Imagine if Miss Cowan visited them and Geoffrey said,

'Why did you bring that woman here? Where on earth did you find her?'

And she would try to explain to him how longingly Miss Cowan had gazed at the armour. But of course he wouldn't be able to understand, ever. How could he be what he was, and also understand?

And Miss Casey who was now exhausted slept and the Wilsons were not speaking to each other and she expected that Geoffrey would say,

'Well, where did you go? Where did you sleep? Whom did you meet? Don't tell me that you didn't meet anyone. It was a stupid idea to go on that bus tour anyway. No one else but you would have done it. Could you not have waited till I got some leave?' No, the thought of the generals and the generals' wives stifled her, with their military kookaburra faces. She wanted to be a kangaroo, to take huge unexpected leaps into the blue. And Miss Casey slept and looked quite old in the dim light of the bus. And Mrs Wilson, she knew, was hostile to her, her secret though smiling enemy. She was keeping Tom from the real joy of his nature. The bars and gratings were everywhere.

The bus travelled on through the evening. The milestones were like little tombstones. Oh how she loved Australia with its mysterious femininity, not at all masculine as she had feared, as she had been led to expect. No, not at all, rather yearning to be itself, as Miss Cowan yearned for articulate speech, as Tom Wilson, large and bearish and funny, yearned to be the person that he really was.

She felt cool and fulfilled as if now she could sing 'Greensleeves': but the moment had passed. She should have sung it when she had the chance. And that young unmarried spectacled girl who worked in the Civil Service was sleeping in the seat directly in front of her. Oh the aboriginal brilliance of this land, its shining bone-like moon, the bone of our common existence, the boomerang moon curved like a horn.

And they all dozed and the bus was silent. Soon they would be back in Canberra and Geoffrey would be waiting for her with the car, and the others would take buses or taxis. And Geoffrey would say

'Everything all right?' And she would be able to say to him that everything was all right except that...

Suddenly she said out of the silence to the four, 'You must really come and visit. I mean it. We must make a date.' But they didn't believe her. So she must make them believe her, she must set a specific date. And into the world of the generals' wives she must bring the harelipped Miss Cowan, the Wilsons from Glasgow, Miss Casey who had once taught pupils in Sydney, and also played the gambling machines. She must bring the wildness into the tame, the lame towards the healthy. She must not let Geoffrey overwhelm her. Nor the generals' wives. She must not be stifled.

'Let's make it June the 5th,' she said consulting her diary, in the dimness, by the light of that unutterably strange moon. 'You must come then.'

And they didn't believe her. And they didn't answer.

'June the 5th then,' she said as she took her case from the rack. And the others were still in the bus gathering their possessions together as she ran out to meet Geoffrey who was waiting for her, stiff and military and young, holding Shirley by the hand.

'How are you, old girl?' he said. But she watched for a while till the other four got out and joined the queue for the taxis, and she waved to them and they waved back. And then she was in the car and still waving.

'Your friends?' said Geoffrey sarcastically as he steered the car away from the bus station. And she said in a very distinct voice,

'Yes. They're coming to see me on June the 5th. I hope you have nothing fixed that evening.' Clutching her koala bear Shirley looked from her mother to her father.

'I must be military too,' thought Daphne. 'I must fight with stiffness in order to allow the flowing to enter.'

And later that night as she lay gazing up into the imperialistic face of her husband she thought, 'June the 5th it must be, will be.' And it seemed to her that she must be like a Ned Kelly and fight it out and this time win, peering out from behind the green slim tree trunks. And on that day perhaps Miss Cowan would learn to speak.

The Travelling Poet

ONE autumn day he stopped at my door. He said he was on a sponsored walk to raise money for a boy who needed medical treatment in America. He was also a poet and as he travelled, he read his poems in pubs, halls. He sold copies of them to pay for his lodgings.

He sat in the living-room and took out a bag with some of the booklets that he had published at his own expense. There were also letters from prominent people: 'Lord X thanks you for letting him see the enclosed but is sorry that he is not able to contribute to your appeal.' 'As you will understand Lady X has many demands on her resources and is sorry that she can only send two pounds at this time.'

His poems were bad. There was also a children's story about a fox which was not much better. He found out that I was a poet and asked for my opinion. I was hypocritical as usual.

It turned out that he had been in prison and that was where he had begun to write. His father had been a crane driver; his mother had been an alcoholic. He himself had been a heavy drinker but had according to himself stopped.

'When I was young,' he said, 'we were very poor. We used to beg for clothes. I have seen myself wearing girls' clothes.'

Imagine that, I thought, girls' clothes.

His wife had left him and gone to America.

'I used to be quite violent when I was young but not any more. I was in prison a few times.' This long journey to raise funds for the boy was in a way a rehabilitation for him.

He had cuttings and photographs from various local papers,

with headlines such as the following: 'Ex-Convict Raises Money for Charity Mission'. And so on. He was very proud of these cuttings, and of his letters on headed notepaper, from the aristocracy, from Members of Parliament. He had even sent a copy of his booklet to Ronald Reagan, to Mrs Thatcher. I thought he had an adamant vanity.

He left me a story about the fox to read at my leisure so that I could give him an opinion on it when he returned.

As he travelled northwards he phoned me every night.

'I feel,' he said, 'as if you are interested, as if I'm in touch with home.' He discovered the luminousness of landscapes (he himself had been brought up in the city). One night he slept in a barn and when he had asked for a clock to get him up in the morning the farmer had told him, 'You have a clock. You wait.' The clock turned out to be a cockerel. 'Imagine that,' he said. He was happy as a sandboy. Another time he saw a fawn crossing the road.

'Tonight,' he phoned, 'I'm booked into the Caledonian Hotel. I shall pay for my room with some booklets of my poems.' He had already raised the almost unbelievable sum of £2000. 'I ask for cheques so that I won't be tempted to drink the money.'

He also said to me, 'I mentioned your name to the landlady but she had never heard of you.'

Actually it bothered me a little that she had never heard of me. It also seemed to me that my visitor had become more dismissive of me, more sure of himself. After all he was not a very good poet, indeed not a poet at all.

Let me also say that I wished he had not come to the door. I had my own routine. I started writing at nine in the morning and finished at four. He had interrupted my routine and also put me in the position of being hypocritical about his poems. I had met people like him before. For instance, here is a story.

Another poet of approximately the same calibre as my visitor had accosted me once in Glasgow. He was unemployed, his wife had left him, he had smashed his car, his father was dying of a stroke, and his mother of cancer; he had been cut by a razor when he was a bouncer in a night club; he had been charged with sexual assault; he had fallen out of the window of a second storey flat after taking drugs. Now it might be considered that such a person might turn out to be a good poet but in fact his poems were very sentimental and didn't reflect his life at all. Such is the unfairness of literature. What can you do for such people who have experienced the intransigence and randomness of the world and cannot make use of it?

My visitor disturbed me. I imagined him as I have said learning the luminousness of the world, coming across pheasants, foxes, deer; rising on frosty mornings among farm steadings; setting out in the dews of autumn; writing his poems ('I have no difficulty at all: I can write four poems a day easy'); meeting people.

One night he phoned me and said that he was going to have an interview with the Duke of —. The local paper had asked to take a photograph of the two of them together.

Alcoholism is a terrible thing. I know a talented man who is in the entertainment world and who often does not turn up at concerts etc. because he has been inveigled into taking a drink. It was really quite noble that this 'poet' was taking his money in cheques so that he would not be tempted into using it to buy drink. Drily he toiled on, changing his poems and booklets into cheques, having as far as I could see nothing much of his own at all.

I can't write. Isn't that odd? Most days when I sit down at my desk I have no difficulty at all in writing something. But from the time that this poet called on me, I have written nothing, I have dried up. I think of him plodding along a dusty road, stopping at a hotel or a boarding house, negotiating with the sharp-eyed owner, paying for his keep with pamphlets, poems. What a quite extraordinary thing. Nevertheless I should have had nothing to do with him. And I am paying for it now. This is the first time I've ever had writer's block. What does it mean?

Maybe he won't come back. He hasn't phoned so often

recently and when he does he sounds more independent, as if the two of us were equals.

Last night he phoned. He had run into another writer in a pub. This writer decorated the wall of his room with rejection slips. He didn't think he was getting fair treatment because he was a Socialist. He dressed in a Wild West outfit. He was 'quite a character'. 'Listen,' I nearly said to my visitor, 'don't be deceived by him. He is a bad writer. I can smell his amateurism a mile away. People like that always dress in an outré manner, they always say that they are not understood. Avoid him. Listen to me instead.'

I started writing when I was about eleven. I believe that routine, hard work is the most important thing in any art. I sit down at my desk every morning at nine. Without a routine all writers and artists are doomed. I have never been an alcoholic. Writing is my life: that must be the case with all artists.

I should have asked him how he had got involved in his walk to raise money for a boy who is dying and is to be sent to America where the 'poet's' wife is. Maybe she left him because he didn't make any money, because he insisted on taking part in such outlandish projects. On the other hand she might have left him when he was in prison. 'They were very good to me in prison. It was there I met the man who illustrated my booklet. I had five hundred printed. Who is your publisher? Do you think you could interest him in my poems, my story about the fox?'

A startling statement he had made was, 'This is all that I have left, my writing.'

When I was younger I actually used to taste the excitement of art. I remember days when myself and my current girlfriend would travel on a green tram in Aberdeen. Mornings were glorious. I used to shout out lines from Shakespearean plays in cemeteries, among the granite. 'The great poet,' I used to say, 'is always on the frontier.'

Later I went back to Aberdeen and had the following fantasy. My earlier self met me on the street wearing a student's cloak. He was with a group of his friends. They passed me in the hard yellow light laughing, and probably never even noticed me. Perhaps they thought of me as a prosperous fat bourgeois. My earlier self didn't recognize me but I knew him. He was as cutting and supercilious as ever.

I don't think my visitor will visit me on his way south. He hasn't phoned for a week now. He is probably lost in admiration for his genuine artistic friend who is so daring. I feel sorry for him. Really he's so innocent with all his talk of cockerels, barns, deer. I am sure he will have another copy of the story of the fox and not ask me for my opinion. Perhaps his companion has heard of me, dismisses me.

Once before my wife left me I saw a small knot of weasels, a mother weasel with her tiny family, crossing the road. They looked like notes in music.

Another thing I have discovered about myself, I hate the cold. And the rain.

Autumn is passing and he hasn't come. I have heard nothing more of him. Perhaps he did after all use some of his money for drinking. Perhaps he has returned to prison. Perhaps he went berserk one night, was arrested. It is not easy to travel alone, and one's wife to be in America. There is no such thing as goodness: aggression must out. The greater the creativity the greater the aggression if thwarted.

It is winter. There is snow on the ground, he certainly won't come now. And I have not written anything for two months. I begin to write and I fail to continue. The reason my wife left me was that she said I didn't speak enough to her, about ordinary things. As a matter of fact I found that I couldn't speak about ordinary things: I would try to think of something to say but couldn't.

Listen, let me tell you a story which I read in some book or other. There was a mathematician in Cambridge who knew that being over forty he could no longer do original work in his field. So he spent his time making up cricket teams to play against each other. One cricket team would have names beginning with B such as Beethoven, Brahms, Balzac. Another one would have names beginning with A such as Joan of Arc, Aristotle, Archimedes. One day he received a letter from India which contained a number of incomprehensible equations, and he threw the letter into the wastepaper basket. However in the afternoon he usually went for a walk with a friend of his (also a mathematician) and he told him about the letter and the equations. The result was that they retrieved them from the wastepaper basket. It turned out that they had been created by a young Indian genius who had never been taught orthodox mathematics. He was taken over to Cambridge and died young. It is said that his last words were, Did you notice that the number plate on the ambulance was a perfect cube?

Now I'm sure that man had no small talk.

Who in fact is the boy and what disease is he dying of? Maybe my visitor faked the whole business in order to make money. But no, I don't think so: the story is true. He showed me a newspaper cutting which described the boy but I didn't read it very carefully. I have difficulty with detail and especially with people's names.

He must by now have collected £3000 with his bad poetry. What an extraordinary thing.

Actually up until the very last moment I didn't believe that my wife would leave me. I used to say to her, You won't find anyone else as interesting as me. She picked up her case and took a bus. And never said another word to me. I waited and waited but she never phoned. I tried to trace her but was unsuccessful. She was quite beautiful: she will find someone.

Actually she used to weep over stories on the TV. She would dab at her eyes or run to the bathroom. At first I didn't realize what was happening.

Every night I gaze up the road before I lock the door. I am waiting for my poet but he never comes. He has become a mythological figure in my mind like the Wandering Jew. His bag is full of undrinkable cheques. His mouth is dry. He cannot afford the money for the phone. All the money that he collects he puts in his bag which swells out like a balloon. Maybe that's it, he can't afford to phone.

Or he has gone home.

Or his wife has come back to him.

Or he has shacked up with his Wild West friend.

Or he has become so stunned by the beauty of the Highlands that he will never leave them again.

And here I am making money out of his wanderings. By means of this story. Whereas he...

I imagine the boy in a hospital in America. He is being watched over by doctors, surgeons. They are all looking at a clock. 'Soon he will come with the money,' they are saying to the boy. 'You must trust him. Till then we can't treat you.' And he swims across the Atlantic with his bag of cheques. He fights waves, he pacifies the ocean with his bad poems. Out of the green water he coins green dollars. And the boy's breathing becomes worse and worse and the doctor says, 'He won't be long now.'

It has begun to snow. He is perhaps out in the snow in the Highlands, perhaps at John O'Groats with his bag. The snow is a white prison round him: he can't even take a nip of whisky. I feel sorry for him. He should come in out of the cold, he has done enough. He has had more courage than me. With his bad poems he has done more than I have with my good ones. I can see that. And he was just as poor as me.

My writer's block has persisted. I think I am finished as a writer.

The snow is falling very gently. A ghost tree clasps the real tree like a bridegroom with a bride. They have had the worst winter in Florida in living memory.

What a sky of stars. And yet I see them as if I was a spectator. I'd better shut the door, he'll never come, my muse in her girl's dress will never come again. I shall have to take account of that.

I heard a story today about a villager. He has run away with a woman much younger than himself and left his wife. It is said that he was the last person anyone would have expected to have done anything like that. What does he hope to gain?

What energy, what a strange leap. Will there not come a time when he will make a third spring and then a fourth one? As if Romeo and Juliet were still alive...

Last night I thought I saw him emerging out of the snow with his bag. When I went to the cat's dish there was a snail eating the food. Unless I take my bag on my shoulders I shall never write again. Unless I am willing to accept the risk of bad poems.

The phone rang but it was a wrong number.

Imagine first of all surviving in girl's clothes and then in bad poems.

I am sure that when the spring comes he will be happier. I can almost hear the ice breaking, the sound of running waters, the cry of the cockerel. The fox shakes itself out of its prison of snow. Meagre and thin. It laps at the fresh water. All around it is the snow with its white undamaged pages.

Mr Heine

IT was ten o'clock at night and Mr Bingham was talking to the mirror. He said 'Ladies and gentlemen,' and then stopped, clearing his throat, before beginning again, 'Headmaster and colleagues, it now forty years since I first entered the teaching profession. – Will that do as a start, dear?'

'It will do as a start, dear,' said his wife Lorna.

'Do you think I should perhaps put in a few jokes?' said her husband anxiously. 'When Mr Currie retired, his speech was well received because he had a number of jokes in it. My speech will be delivered in one of the rooms of the Domestic Science Department where they will have tea and scones prepared. It will be after class hours.'

'A few jokes would be acceptable,' said his wife, 'but I think that the general tone should be serious.'

Mr Bingham squared his shoulders, preparing to address the mirror again, but at that moment the doorbell rang.

'Who can that be at this time of night?' he said irritably.

'I don't know, dear. Shall I answer it?'

'If you would, dear.'

His wife carefully laid down her knitting and went to the door. Mr Bingham heard a murmur of voices and after a while his wife came back into the living room with a man of perhaps forty-five or so who had a pale rather haunted face, but who seemed eager and enthusiastic and slightly jaunty.

'You won't know me,' he said to Mr Bingham. 'My name is Heine. I am in advertising. I compose little jingles such as the following:

When your dog is feeling depressed
Give him Dalton's. It's the best.
I used to be in your class in 1944-5. I heard you were retiring
so I came along to offer you my felicitations.'

'Oh?' said Mr Bingham turning away from the mirror
regretfully.

'Isn't that nice of Mr Heine?' said his wife.

'Won't you sit down?' she said and Mr Heine sat down,
carefully pulling up his trouser legs so that he wouldn't crease
them.

'My landlady of course has seen you about the town,' he
said to Mr Bingham. 'For a long time she thought you were
a farmer. It shows one how frail fame is. I think it is because
of your red healthy face. I told her you had been my English
teacher for a year. Now I am in advertising. One of my best
rhymes is:

Dalton's Dogfood makes your collie
Obedient and rather jolly.

You taught me Tennyson and Pope. I remember both rather
well.'

'The fact,' said Mr Bingham, 'that I don't remember you
says nothing against you personally. Thousands of pupils have
passed through my hands. Some of them come to speak to
me now and again. Isn't that right dear?'

'Yes,' said Mrs Bingham, 'that happens quite regularly.'

'Perhaps you could make a cup of coffee, dear,' said Mr
Bingham and when his wife rose and went into the kitchen,
Mr Heine leaned forward eagerly.

'I remember that you had a son,' he said. 'Where is he now?'

'He is in educational administration,' said Mr Bingham
proudly. 'He has done well.'

'When I was in your class,' said Mr Heine, 'I was eleven or
twelve years old. There was a group of boys who used to
make fun of me. I don't know whether I have told you but I
am a Jew. One of the boys was called Colin. He was taller
than me, and fair-haired.'

'You are not trying to insinuate that it was my son,' said

Mr Bingham angrily. 'His name was Colin but he would never do such a thing. He would never use physical violence against anyone.'

'Well,' said Mr Heine affably. 'It was a long time ago, and in any case

> The past is past and for the present
> It may be equally unpleasant.

Colin was the ringleader, and he had blue eyes. In those days I had a lisp which sometimes returns in moments of nervousness. Ah, there is Mrs Bingham with the coffee. Thank you, madam.'

'Mr Heine says that when he was in school he used to be terrorized by a boy called Colin who was fair-haired,' said Mr Bingham to his wife.

'It is true,' said Mr Heine, 'but as I have said it was a long time ago and best forgotten about. I was small and defenceless and I wore glasses. I think, Mrs Bingham, that you yourself taught in the school in those days.'

'Sugar?' said Mrs Bingham. 'Yes. As it was during the war years and most of the men were away I taught Latin. My husband was deferred.'

'*Amo, amas, amat*,' said Mr Heine. 'I remember I was in your class as well.'

'I was not a memorable child,' he added, stirring his coffee reflectively, 'so you probably won't remember me either. But I do remember the strong rhymes of Pope which have greatly influenced me. And so, Mr Bingham, when I heard you were retiring I came along as quickly as my legs would carry me, without tarrying. I am sure that you chose the right profession. I myself have chosen the right profession. You, sir, though you did not know it at the time placed me in that profession.'

Mr Bingham glanced proudly at his wife.

'I remember the particular incident very well,' said Mr Heine. 'You must remember that I was a lonely little boy and not good at games.

> Keeping wicket was not cricket.
> Bat and ball were not for me suitable at all.

And then again I was being set upon by older boys and given a drubbing every morning in the boiler room before classes commenced. The boiler room was very hot. I had a little talent in those days, not much certainly, but a small poetic talent. I wrote verses which in the general course of things I kept secret. Thus it happened one afternoon that I brought them along to show you, Mr Bingham. I don't know whether you will remember the little incident, sir.'

'No,' said Mr Bingham, 'I can't say that I do.'

'I admired you, sir, as a man who was very enthusiastic about poetry, especially Tennyson. That is why I showed you my poems. I remember that afternoon very well. It was raining heavily and the room was indeed so gloomy that you asked one of the boys to switch on the lights. You said, "Let's have some light on the subject, Hughes." I can remember Hughes quite clearly, as indeed I can remember your quips and jokes. In any case Hughes switched on the lights and it was a grey day, not in May but in December, an ember of the done sun in the sky. You read one of my poems. As I say, I can't remember it now but it was not in rhyme. "Now I will show you the difference between good poetry and bad poetry," you said, comparing my little effort with Tennyson's work, which was mostly in rhyme. When I left the room I was surrounded by a pack of boys led by blue-eyed fair-haired Colin. The moral of this story is that I went into advertising and therefore into rhyme. It was a revelation to me.

> A revelation straight from God
> That I should rhyme as I was taught.

So you can see, sir, that you are responsible for the career in which I have flourished.'

'I don't believe it, sir,' said Mr Bingham furiously.

'Don't believe what, sir?'

'That that ever happened. I can't remember it.'

'It was Mrs Gross my landlady who saw the relevant passage about you in the paper. I must go immediately, I told her. You thought he was a farmer but I knew differently. That man does not know the influence he has had on his scholars.

That is why I came,' he said simply.

'Tell me, sir,' he added, 'is your son married now?'

'Colin?'

'The same, sir.'

'Yes, he's married. Why do you wish to know?'

'For no reason, sir. Ah, I see a photograph on the mantelpiece. In colour. It is a photograph of the bridegroom and the bride.

> How should we not hail the blooming bride
> With her good husband at her side?

What is more calculated to stabilize a man than marriage? Alas I never married myself. I think I never had the confidence for such a beautiful institution. May I ask the name of the fortunate lady?'

'Her name is Norah,' said Mrs Bingham sharply. 'Norah Mason.'

'Well, well,' said Mr Heine enthusiastically. 'Norah, eh? We all remember Norah, don't we? She was a lady of free charm and great beauty. But I must not go on. All those unseemly pranks of childhood which we should consign to the dustbins of the past. Norah Mason, eh?' and he smiled brightly. 'I am so happy that your son has married Norah.'

'Look here,' said Mr Bingham, raising his voice.

'I hope that my felicitations, congratulations, will be in order for them too, I sincerely hope so, sir. Tell me, did your son Colin have a scar on his brow which he received as a result of having been hit on the head by a cricket ball.'

'And what if he had?' said Mr Bingham.

'Merely the sign of recognition, sir, as in the Greek tragedies. My breath in these days came in short pants, sir, and I was near-sighted. I deserved all that I got. And now sir, forgetful of all that, let me say that my real purpose in coming here was to give you a small monetary gift which would come particularly from myself and not from the generality. My salary is a very comfortable one. I thought of something in the region of... Oh look at the time. It is nearly half-past eleven at night.

> At eleven o'clock at night
> The shades come out and then they fight.

I was, as I say, thinking of something in the order of...'

'Get out, sir,' said Mr Bingham angrily. 'Get out, sir, with your insinuations. I do not wish to hear any more.'

'I beg your pardon,' said Mr Heine in a wounded voice.

'I said "Get out, sir." It is nearly midnight. Get out.'

Mr Heine rose to his feet. 'If that is the way you feel, sir. I only wished to bring my felicitations.'

'We do not want your felicitations,' said Mrs Bingham. 'We have enough of them from others.'

'Then I wish you both goodnight and you particularly, Mr Bingham as you leave the profession you have adorned for so long.'

'GET OUT, sir,' Mr Bingham shouted, the veins standing out on his forehead.

Mr Heine walked slowly to the door, seemed to wish to stop and say something else, but then changed his mind and the two left in the room heard the door being shut.

'I think we should both go to bed, dear,' said Mr Bingham panting heavily.

'Of course, dear,' said his wife. She locked the door and said, 'Will you put the lights out or shall I?'

'You may put them out, dear,' said Mr Bingham. When the lights had been switched off they stood for a while in the darkness, listening to the little noises of the night from which Mr Heine had so abruptly and outrageously come.

'I can't remember him. I don't believe he was in the school at all,' said Mrs Bingham decisively.

'You are right, dear,' said Mr Bingham who could make out the outline of his wife in the half-darkness. 'You are quite right, dear.'

'I have a good memory and I should know,' said Mrs Bingham as they lay side by side in the bed. Mr Bingham heard the cry of the owl, throatily soft, and turned over and was soon fast asleep. His wife listened to his snoring, staring sightlessly at the objects and furniture of the bedroom which she had gathered with such persistence and passion over the years.

The Scream

THE play lasted about an hour and took place in a small theatre off the High St in Edinburgh. The story of the play was not complicated. A prison had been burnt down in the night and there was an enquiry as to who had done it. The cast was as follows:

The Governor – an idealist who hated brutality.
The Governor's wife – who supported her husband as an honourable man but was also sex-starved.
Two brutal guards – one tall and one small. They had ill-treated the prisoners, made them bend down and eat their own excrement. In the presence of the Governor, however, they always appeared reasonable and respectful, having only the welfare of the prisoners at heart!
There was a cleaner who appeared at times dim-witted but at other times could discuss Marx: a homosexual prisoner who was beaten up by the guards in a scene of great cruelty: the man who headed the enquiry who was an ex-communist, drank a great deal and was in love with his secretary, a not particularly good-looking girl of great idealism: and finally a boy who had left Cambridge and who found himself plunged into 'real life'.

The audience liked the play. It started slowly and then built up to a claustrophobic denouement. But the enquiry didn't discover who had burnt the prison down.

The part of the homosexual was acted by Jeff Coates, a young actor from Cambridge. In the pivotal scene he was fitted up with electrodes while the two guards tortured him.

One of their lines was 'the poof of the pudding is in the eating.' For the two guards were intellectuals too, clever, cunning, able to switch from viciousness to calm collected discussion especially when the Governor appeared, the Governor, tortured by moral doubts, whom they despised. After all what was a prison for but to convert criminals to goodness by torture?

Jeff Coates was changed by the play. At first he had not liked it very much. He thought the dialogue at times brittle, its poeticisms brilliant but perhaps esoteric. But gradually it took a grip of him, he felt himself inside a world of almost total evil. At coffee breaks he would speak only to the Governor and never to the guards. In the crucial scene he screamed a high piercing scream though of course it was only a pretence of torture he was suffering. At times however he felt he was being really tortured.

The trouble was that he was really a homosexual and that made it worse – or did it? He couldn't make up his mind. Was it indeed worse to be a real homosexual in that scene? (Also in the play he was attacked by prisoners.) He sometimes felt that the two guards really hated him, for neither was a homosexual. They made comments about his walk and these comments he accepted as belonging to the play. The women in the cast befriended him more than the men did, though of course he was not interested in them sexually. In the scene where he was being tortured he felt real hatred emanating from the two guards as if they were his most bitter enemies. Of course he had experience of being beaten up in real life, particularly in a public convenience in London, about two years before.

His scream was real, he thought, because it came from the centre of his being. And yet it was happening in a play. These men didn't really hate him, he told himself, they were merely acting, they obviously had to act as if they hated him. The Governor too in real life was stingy, sarcastic, embittered, not at all attractive. The two guards in real life were not at all intellectual: in fact he despised them. For he himself had read Artaud on the Theatre of Cruelty. The stage became very small each night. It shrank. Every night he waited to be tortured. It was almost as if that was the reason for his existence.

As time passed he became more and more solitary, arriving late, leaving early. He didn't want to see these contemptuous eyes nor did he wish to listen to the banal conversation of the guards. The scream was taking a lot out of him, he had to prepare himself for it, it shattered his whole being so that if there had been glass near him it would have cracked. He didn't wish to discuss the play with the others since in his opinion they didn't really know what it was about, they did not know what suffering was. Of course none of them had ever suffered except in fantasy. That at any rate was what he thought. He himself had suffered, especially on the day that his mother had discovered him in bed with a male friend of his. That was the worst. Her whole face had disintegrated: he would always remember that moment.

O none of them had really suffered. He himself had suffered, however. He was the one who was in the prison. The suffering was disguised by talk about morality, about Marx, but nothing could disguise the torture. And his scream, was it real or not? For after all he wasn't really being tortured. In fact the two guards used to make a point of asking him over to take coffee with them. He was probably making a mistake in thinking that they hated him.

And he loved acting. He had acted many other parts as well as the part he was acting in this play. That was the awful and marvellous thing about actors, that they took on themselves the pains and sufferings of others. They brought to audiences the calmness of art at the expense of their own tortured spirits. He had acted kings, drunks, and most especially the dark blind figure in *The Room*, by Pinter. And in all these instances he had sought determinedly for the meaning of the text. When he was acting the part of Creon, he had thought, This city of Edinburgh is Thebes, we shall show it its plague, though there was in fact no appearance of plague in Edinburgh's theatrical façade, with its green light shining about the castle at night.

To be an actor was to be a healer, a doctor. And the scream waited for him every night. In fact he had become obsessed by it.

He stayed in lodgings on his own. Every night he left the theatre and walked to them through the throbbing festival city, through the slums of the High St. After the scream he strolled through the streets, emptied of emotion, solitary. And he thought, the guards are at least uncomplicated. They are brutal, they have assessed the world as it really is. They had no imagination, they could not put themselves in the position of the weak, nor did they want to. He found himself hating them in return. Why had they taken these parts unless they were in a deep way suited to them? And this in spite of the fact that such an idea was stupid.

And as for the governor, he despised him. The governor had never protected him. There he was tortured every day while the governor stood around like a moral priggish Brutus and the guards like Mark Antonies ran rings round him. They would spring to attention while prisoners bled in the cells. O how they laughed at that poor tortured libertarian in the burnt prison under the open sky! Who had burnt the prison? Was it perhaps the governor himself? Or his wife? Or the cleaner who could discuss Marx.

And every night his own high scream was the peak point of the play. It rose to a crescendo, then died away to a whisper, to exhaustion. And the audience winced (or perhaps they loved it. Who could tell?) But none of them was unaffected. He saw to that. And when the play was over and the audience had left, he and the other actors would have their coffee and discuss the effectiveness of the night's work. And it became more and more demanding to create the scream. It wasn't easy to scream like that every night.

One night he waited behind till the others had gone. Then he went out into the street. It was a Saturday night and the air was mild. All round him he sensed the delirium of the Festival. There were lovers strolling hand in hand, there were men in strange colourful costumes, the world itself was a theatre. It was Romeo and Juliet he saw sitting on a bench, it was the old woman from *Crime and Punishment* who staggered drunkenly down the street. The city was a theatre at which the plague had not struck.

He walked with his usual mincing walk. He had never been conscious of it himself but he had been told of it. Actually he was still wearing his prison clothes for he hadn't bothered changing. Well, why shouldn't he? One night he had seen a tall man in a black gown walking towards him on stilts, with a skull instead of a face.

He now entered a street which was quite dark. The council was dimming its lamps in certain areas even during the Festival.

And then they were there. There must have been about six of them. They were wearing green scarves and they were shouting. They owned the street. They were like members of a crowd in one of Shakespeare's plays, perhaps *Julius Caesar*: but they were really vicious. It might be that their team had lost. Who knew? He and they were in the dim street together and they were marching towards him. Perhaps he should run? He thought about it but he didn't run. They were chanting. Their heads were shaved.

Poof, they shouted, poof they shouted again. They danced around him. Poof in his theatrical clothes. And they with their shaved heads on which Union Jacks had been painted. (One light in the alley like a spot light showed this to him.)

It had happened before. It would happen again. Those without imagination were upon him. The animals with their teeth.

Poof, they shouted, bloody poof. And then they were on him and beat him to the ground and trampled on him. And his glasses fell off and cracked, he could feel that. He looked upwards but he could hardly see them. All he could see was a kaleidoscope of colour. And he could smell the smell of alcohol. And then he screamed. And as he screamed the high piercing scream they ran away and left him in a quick scurry.

And he lay there on the street alone, listening to the noise they made as they left, and he thought, That scream, was it different? Was it different from the one in the play? Which was the real scream and which was the unreal one? The prepared or the unprepared? The, as it were, artistic one or the real one? And he thought, the artistic one was the real one. This was only an accidental one. This was not the scream of art, this was the one he had attracted by walking like a poof and taking that lane which he should not have taken and continuing to walk towards them as perhaps he should not have done. Had he been trying to learn more about the artistic scream by this one? He felt naked in the dim street without his glasses.

He would have to make his way back to his real landlady. And with his real face. And put ointment on his real bruises.

He staggered a little as he stood up, coming out of the scream. Everything was silent around him. No one had heard him. There had been no audience. How therefore could his scream have been more real than the theatrical one?

How?

The Old Woman, the Baby and Terry

THE fact was that the old woman wanted to live. All her faculties, her energies, were shrunken down to that desire. She drew everything into herself so that she could live, survive. It was obscene, it was a naked obscenity.

'Do you know what she's doing now?' said Harry to his wife Eileen. 'She keeps every cent. She hoards her pension, she's taken to hiding her money in the pillow slips, under blankets. She reminds me of someone, I can't think who.'

'But what can we do?' said Eileen, who was expecting a baby.

Harry worked with a Youth Organization. He earned £7,000 a year. There was one member of the organization called Terry MacCallum who, he thought, was insane. Terry had tried to rape one of the girls on the snooker table one night. He was a psychopath. Yet Harry wanted to save him. He hated it when he felt that a case was hopeless.

'She won't even pay for a newspaper,' said Harry.

'I know,' said Eileen. 'This morning I found her taking the cigarette stubs from the bucket.'

The child jumped in her womb. She loved Harry more than ever: he was patient and kind. But he grew paler every day: his work was so demanding and Terry MacCallum was so mad and selfish.

'I've never met anyone like him,' said Harry. 'His selfishness is a talent, a genius. It's diamond hard, it shines. I should get rid of him, I know that. Also he's drunk a lot of the time. He said to me yesterday, I don't care for anyone. I'm a bastard, you know that. I'm a scrounger, I hate everyone.'

Harry couldn't understand Terry. Everything that was done for him he accepted and then kicked you in the teeth. He was a monster. He haunted his dreams.

The child kicked in Eileen's womb. She wanted it badly. She had a hunger for it. She wanted it to suck her breasts, she wanted it to crawl about the room, she wanted it to make her alive again.

And all the time the old lady hoarded her banknotes. One day Eileen mentioned to her that they needed bread but she ignored hints of any kind. She even hoarded the bread down the sides of her chair. She tried to borrow money from Eileen. She sang to herself. She gathered her arms around herself, she was like a plant that wouldn't die. Eileen shuddered when she looked at her. She thought that she was sucking her life from her but not like the baby. The baby throve, it milked her, it grew and grew. She was like a balloon, she thrust herself forward like a ship. Her body was like a ship's prow.

'I tried talking to him,' said Harry. 'I can't talk to him at all. He doesn't understand. I can't communicate. He admits everything, he thinks that the world should look after him. He wants everything, he has never grown up. I have never in my life met such selfishness. If he feels sexy he thinks that a woman should put out for him immediately. If he feels hungry he thinks that other people should feed him. I am kind to him but he hates me. What can you do with those who don't see? Is there a penance for people like that? What do you do with those who can't understand?

The baby moved blindly in her womb, instinctively, strategically. She said to Harry, 'I'm frightened. Today I thought that the ferns were gathering round the house, that they wanted to eat me. I think we should cut the ferns down.'

'Not in your condition,' said Harry. He looked thin, besieged.

The old lady said, 'I don't know why you married him. He doesn't make much money, does he? Why doesn't he move to the city? He could make more money there.' She hid a tea bag in her purse. And a biscuit.

The child moved in the womb. It was a single mouth that sucked. Blood, milk, it sucked. It grew to be like its mother. It sang a song of pure selfishness. It had stalks like fern. The stars at night sucked dew from the earth. The sun dried the soil. Harry had the beak of a seagull.

'Last night he wouldn't get off the snooker table,' said Harry. 'There are others who want to play, I said to him. This is my snooker table, he said. It isn't, I said. It is, he said. You try and take it off me. And then he said, Lend me five pounds. No, I said. Why, he said. Because you're selfish, I said. I'm not, he said. I'm a nice fellow, everyone says so. I've got a great sense of humour. What do you do with someone like that? I can't get through to him at all. And yet I must.'

'What for?' said Eileen.

'I just have to.'

'You never will,' said Eileen.

'Why not?'

'Just because. Nature is like that. I don't want the child.'

'What?'

'I know what I mean. Nature is like that. I don't want the child.'

Harry had nightmares. He was on an operating table. A doctor waas introducing leeches into his veins. The operating table was actually for playing snooker on. It had a green velvet surface. He played with a baby's small head for a ball.

The ferns closed in. In the ferns she might find pound notes. She began to eat bits of coal, stones, crusts. She gnawed at them hungrily. The old lady wouldn't sleep at night. She took to locking her door. What if something happened? They would have to break the door down.

The baby sucked and sucked. Its strategies were imperative. It was like a bee sucking at a flower with frantic hairy legs, its head buried in the blossom, its legs working.

Terry stole some money after the disco. He insisted it was his.

'You lied to me,' said Harry.

'I didn't lie.'

'You said you were at home. I phoned your parents. They said you were out. You lied to me.'

'I didn't lie.'

'But can't you see you said one thing and it wasn't the truth. Can you not see that you lied?'

'I didn't lie.'

'For Christ's sake are you mad. You did lie. What do you think a lie is? Can't you see it?'

'I didn't lie.'

'You'll have to go.'

The old lady had a pile of tea-bags, quarter pounds of butter, cheese, in a bag under the bed.

'You owe me,' she said to Eileen. 'For all those years you owe me. I saw in the paper today that it takes ten thousand pounds to rear a child. You owe me ten thousand pounds. It said that in the paper.'

'You haven't paid for that paper,' said Eileen. 'I've tried my best, don't you understand? How can you be so thick?'

'You owe me ten thousand pounds,' said the old lady in the same monotonous grudging voice. 'It said in the paper. I read it.'

'You are taking my beauty away from me,' said Eileen to the baby. 'You are sucking me dry. You are a leech. You are Dracula. You have blood on your lips. And you don't care.'

She carried the globe in front of her. It had teeth painted all over it.

Harry became thinner and thinner. I must make Terry understand, he kept saying. He must be made to understand, he has never in his whole life given anything to anyone. I won't let him go till I have made him understand. It would be too easy to get rid of him.

Put him out, said Eileen, abort him.

What did you say?

Abort him.

You said abort. I'm frightened.

'Can't you see,' said Eileen. 'That's what it is. People feed and feed. Cows feed on grass, grass feeds on bones, bones feed on other bones. It's a system. The whole world is like a mouth. Blake was wrong. It's not a green and pleasant land at all. The rivers are mouths. The sun is the biggest mouth of all.'

'Are you all right, Eileen?'

'Oh hold me,' said Harry.

And they clung together in the night. But Eileen said, 'Look at the ceiling. Do you see it? It's a spider.' It hung like a black pendant. A moth swam towards the light from the darkness outside. The spider was a patient engineer. Suddenly Eileen stood on top of the bed and ripped the web apart. Bastard, she said. Go and find something else to do. The spider had chubby fists. It was a motheaten pendant.

Terry the psychopath smiled and smiled. He bubbled with laughter.

'Give me,' he said to his mother, 'ten pounds of my birthday money in advance.'

'No.'

'Why not? You were going to give it to me anyway.'

'And what are you going to give me for my birthday?'

'I'll think of something.'

'You won't give me anything, will you? Not a thing will you give me!'

The old woman stole sausages from the fridge, matches from the cupboard. She borrowed cigarettes from Eileen. The latter gazed at her in wonderment, testing how far she would go. The old woman began to wear three coats all at the one time. She tried to go to the bathroom as little as possible: she was hoarding her pee.

'The old woman will live forever,' Eileen screamed. 'She will never die. She will take me with her to the grave. She will hoard me. She will tie string round me, and take me with her to the grave. And the innocent selfish ferns will spring from me. And the baby will feed head down in it, its legs working.'

'No,' she said to Harry, 'I don't want to.'
  'Why not? What's wrong with you?'
  'I don't want to. It's like the bee.'
  'What bee?'
  'The bee, I tell you.'
  'For Christ's sake,' he said. The bee sucked at her body. It sucked her breasts in a huge wandering fragrance.

'I don't know you,' said her mother. 'Who are you? Are you the insurance lady? I'm not giving you any more money. You're after all my money. Are you the coalman? Eileen should pay for that. She owes me ten thousand pounds. I saw that in the paper.'
  'It will cost ten thousand pounds,' Eileen said to Harry.
  'What will?'
  'The baby. To bring it up. It was in the paper. I don't want to have it. It will want its own snooker table. It will smile and smile and be a villain.'

'You will have to go,' Harry told Terry.
  'What for?'
  'Because I can't do anything with you.'
  'What do you mean? You'll be sorry.'
  'Are you threatening me?'
  'No, I'm not threatening you. But you'll be sorry. You'll wake up one day and say to yourself: Did I destroy that boy?' And Terry began to cry.
  'You won't get anything out of me that way,' said Harry. 'I can see through your tricks. You will have to go.'
  'All right. But you'll be sorry. You'll hate yourself.'

'I failed but he went,' said Harry to Eileen. 'And he started
to cry before he went. Oh he's so cunning. But there comes
a time.'

'A time?'

'Yes, a time to save oneself. It's a duty. I see that now. She
will have to go.'

'She?'

'Yes. She'll have to go. There comes a time. I made a mistake. I shall have to act.'

'Act?'

'That's it. Act. She will simply have to go. We can't afford
her.'

'What do you mean?'

'What I say. You've done enough. This is not asked of us.
I can see that now. Tell her she will have to go.'

'You tell her.'

'Right. I'll tell her.'

The two of them were alone. The house seemed to close in
on them.

'What's that?' she said.

'What?'

'The phone,' she said.

'It isn't the phone. You're imagining things. The phone
isn't ringing.'

'Yes it is.'

'No, it isn't.'

The ferns shut off the light. The floor was a huge beach of
sand. She saw the child crossing it towards her. It smiled.

'I love you,' she said.

'I love you,' she repeated.

'The Club is quieter now,' he said. 'Ever since he left. We
know where we are. I'm putting on weight.

'Yes, I see that.'

'It's much quieter. He kept us on our toes. Everyone is
obedient.'

'Yes.'

The child cried.

'I love you,' she said. The circle closed again. The baby smiled and smiled and laughed and laughed. It wobbled on unsteady legs among the ferns.

'I'm wounded,' she said, 'between the legs. Between the legs.' And its hairy head blossomed there. 'Between the legs. I'm wounded,' she said.

In the operating theatre on the snooker table its wild cry came towards her. She cradled the globe of its wet head, which had streamed out of the earth. Her hands closed, opened.

'I love you,' she said. 'There's nothing else for it.'

The phone rang. There was heavy breathing. 'You'll be sorry,' said a voice.

'He never gives up,' said Harry. 'But I don't care.'

'He has become remorseless,' she thought. 'We have been infected.' And she clutched the baby's head to her breast. 'We inherit the disease,' she thought. The baby warbled in its own kingdom. 'Isn't he beautiful?' she said.

'Yes.'

And the baby burbled like an unintelligible phone.

On the Train

IT was late at night when the train stopped at the platform and he boarded it. It seemed to be crowded with people of different races and colours, but there wasn't much noise or din. On the wall of his carriage was a painting by Constable, and on the other was a flyblown mirror. It was as if he had been waiting for this train for most of his life, though its destination was unknown.

As time passed, the light brightened the countryside through which the train was passing. Cows could be seen chewing grass in the fields, smoke rose from the houses straight into the sky. The train stopped at a station called Descartes, at one called Hume, and at another called Locke. Sometimes the stations appeared bright and colourful with little gardens, and on the platforms stood small pompous stationmasters with brightly polished buttons, and large watches in the fobs of their jackets. At other times the stations were striped with shade and light.

Now and again he would stroll down the corridor and look in through the doors of carriages. He would see men and women locked in each other's arms, or a man seated silently by his wife, staring ahead of him, or another reading a book quietly as if there were no one in the whole world but himself. Sometimes there was music on the train, sometimes not. Rabbis, ministers, gurus, many of them with beards, inhabited some of the carriages. He clutched his ticket as the train raced on through the bright sunlight.

For most of the journey the land looked clean and tidy,

divided up into small farms and crofts. A reasonable sun shone on it. People sometimes waved at them from the fields, women with kerchiefs, many of them red or green, the men wearing caps. Once he thought he saw a man and woman in a glade and he could have sworn they were naked. At another time he saw a man wearing only a pair of bright yellow wellingtons fishing in a stream.

He thought of Death as a man with a scythe strolling among the land, perfectly natural, perfectly happy and contented. He would knock on a door and be welcomed like a long-lost exile. He would sit down at a table and be offered food. But later he became dim and smoky and his face could not be distinguished. And people would not let him into the house at all, as if he were a being from another planet, a hated stranger.

More stations passed, one called Leibnitz, then two called Kafka and Kierkegaard respectively. On the tops of hills he could see castles with parks winding around them; mornings sang and sparkled and so did afternoons. Children played and at other times carried huge books about with them like gravestones. They gazed at the smoke which was like transient breath.

He was aware of a man who was joking in a loud voice to his friends in the adjacent carriage. He seemed to have an immense fund of stories. 'When I was in the army,' he said, 'we were prevented from going to church on a Sunday by this corporal. So I hit him. I pushed his head into a barrel of water, and they sent me to Colchester. There I had to run everywhere between two policemen. I thought the most Christian thing was to hit him so that he would let us go to church,' and he laughed. 'I never liked authority much, but I'll tell you that corporal was sent to Easter Island after that. They got rid of him.'

He had many other stories, some of which involved playing practical jokes on a strict aunt of his.

And the train raced on. Sometimes there would be white men standing on the platforms, sometimes a Negro reading *The Times*, or an Indian reading a book. In another carriage he heard two philosophers arguing, one maintaining that children's programmes were the best on television. 'I never miss any of them,' he said. ' "Jackanory" is my favourite one.' His fellow philosopher gazed at him in horror. A tall man with a very narrow head talked about structuralism. Someone else compared *Treasure Island* with Marx's *Das Kapital*. He used the word 'precisely' a lot. He would say, 'It is precisely Squire Trelawney who is the most important person in the book.'

An African who spoke with an Oxford accent complained about his son. 'I told him if he didn't like the food he could leave the house.'

Time passed and he clutched his ticket more tightly. Some of the stations showed clocks which had stopped. Their faces blank and empty. There was a smell of mortality on the train. The evening was falling and he felt that his destination was approaching. He took his case down from the rack, excited by the thought. It was about another hour, however, before the train came to a gliding stop. On the platform were a number of soldiers wearing helmets which looked grey in the fading light.

'Come,' they said. 'Follow us.'

He grew more and more excited. At least something was happening. A gun was put in his hand and he found himself firing it indiscriminately into the crowds which were pouring from the train. People fell onto the platform, writhing with pain. He wanted to feel the pain. It seemed to him that he had read about people like himself who were perfectly happy doing what he was doing. Bang, bang went the gun and more and more people fell down. It was all very banal; there seemed no connection between his gun and their act of falling down. The world didn't change much, that was the extraordinary thing. Pop, pop went the gun and there was this contingent but not necessary flowering of blood. It was all quite ordinary. Even death was a cheat and didn't seem tragic or interesting at all. He opened his mouth and began to howl like a wolf. He jabbed sharp pins into his eyes till blood spurted down his beard. He jabbed and jabbed at his eyes while the train hissed behind him and he was enveloped in a cloud of sighing steam.

The Survivor

THE survivor stood among the debris. There passed by him
a ragged line of refugees with their possessions in carts. They
stared straight ahead of them. Houses were burning, ash was
being blown by a small dry wind.

The survivor stood perfectly still. He passed his hand across
his body to test if he was really there. Yes, he was intact, and
there was no blood on him. A jet screeched across the sky
leaving a thin line behind it. He touched the back of his neck
where the hat had left a hot sweaty mark. It seemed to him
that the trail left by the jet and the mark on the back of his
neck were related in some way.

As he watched the refugees he wondered why he was still
alive. Their carts had red wheels: they were carrying their
bloodied household gods with them. Why were they going
from one place to another? It would be the same everywhere,
wouldn't it? The whole world would surely vibrate with din,
with pain.

He stared down at the headless body of a child. It seemed
as obvious and as unusual as a stone. The ruin seemed normal,
he could hardly remember when it had been otherwise. There
had been soldiers racing about in trucks in their olive-green
uniforms. They had taken out guns and shot people and then
they had raced away again. They barked orders as if they knew
exactly what they were doing, what they wanted. In situations
like this it was perhaps best if one knew what one was doing.

Why me, he asked the sky above him. Why was I selected?
And the question was unanswerable. There were millions and

millions of people in the world and he had survived. He rubbed his face. It was still there. The headless body of the child didn't trouble him now as it did before. At least you are dead, he thought, you will have no further decisions to make – if you ever made any. He himself found it hard to make decisions. Why should he head north rather than south, west rather than east?

But in fact he found that he was heading west, away from the sun. For no reason that he could think of. He came across a tank lying on its side amongst a bank of flowers. It seemed as if the flowers were growing out of the tank. He stared at it for a long time, considering. Some lines came into his head:

> The green tank grew among flowers
> while the sun shone blindly.

But he didn't pursue the poem.

In the distance he could hear the sound of guns, thump after thump. Subconsciously he had walked away from them and that was why he was heading west.

I am a survivor, he thought, there must be a reason for that. Look at all the people who have been shot, bludgeoned to death, hacked, bombed . . . and here am I, alive.

He had taken off his hat and thrown it in a ditch. He was not recognisable as belonging to any side, any party. Blandly the sun shone blue above him. It was exactly the same as on the morning before all the attacks began.

He proceeded on his way, since there was nothing else to do. A big fat man with documents in his hand was running about shouting. 'Look,' he said, 'this is my visa. Everything is in order.' He stared into the survivor's eyes as if pleading with him. 'Tell me that I have done the right thing.' The survivor turned away. The fat man was weeping, turning out his pockets, offering him money. He thinks I am in charge, thought the survivor.

A week ago he had been sitting in a class in the open being lectured to by soldiers in olive-green uniforms. They had told him and others that they must learn to change their attitudes, support the regime. There were a lot of flags.

And then this class had been attacked out of the sky, and there was no one to tell him what he should do or what regime he should belong to. All around him now was a silence which palpitated with fear and hatred.

He stared into the mouth of an open cannon. He went up to it and examined it. Its mouth was big, as if it would swallow him. Its body was shiny. He stroked it absently. He noticed that it was now cold. Its blunt solidity gave it a better right to be there than he had. It was fixed and unwavering in its place.

He saw white flowers in the hedges. They also were more authoritative than he was in his white shirt. They frothed and foamed with the life that was in them. They too extended their empire.

Below him on the ground he saw a snail with its aerials extended. He banged his foot on the ground in front of it and it came to a halt. Poor snail, he thought. You hear something but you don't know what it is. I shouldn't really be banging the ground like this, frightening you. The snail was velvety black. Its aerials were its only defences.

He walked on, leaving the snail behind him. In the distance he could see flames rising and falling, but there was no noise coming from them. People were burning among these flames, jumping out of windows perhaps, but there was only the silence. And he touched himself again: yes, I am here. My stomach has not been gutted, I have not been beheaded, though I have seen many beheaded with great curved swords. Who are these people who behead others? What kind of people are they? Maybe they don't realize what they are doing. Maybe they don't think as I do. Maybe they can't imagine what it's like to be beheaded, to suffer pain. Maybe they are burning with faith. I, on the contrary, have no faith at all. Maybe it is better to have faith and behead people than to have no faith at all. It is hard for me to feel the reality of things. Maybe the stones will shift and move eventually like clouds.

He remembered in the class a little man who had stared at him vindictively as if he hated him. What have I done to that

man, he asked himself. The man had hit him across the face
and prodded him with a bayonet. The bruise was still on his
cheek. Why had the small busy man done that? He couldn't
understand it. And yet the hatred had been as palpable as
stench. Maybe he himself had a smell to which the soldier
had responded with enmity. A smell of nothingness, of unreal-
ity.

He came to a fragment of wall. Set in the wall there was a
face, a Roman face, arrogant and haughty. The face stared out
at him with dazzling cruelty as if he weren't there. The eyes
were cold, empty. The head was proud, indifferent. It was
like the face of an emperor. He touched the eyes gently, but
not before he had seen some small busy animal running out
of the wall and across what appeared to be an empty courtyard.

He came to a grassy verge along which he walked. He stopped when he saw a small blue flower there. He touched it
gently as he had touched the sculptured face. It was tiny, beautiful, hermit-like. It was saying: I wish to be alone, quiet, studi-
ous. Its petals were indescribably soft. That was how I used
to be, thought the survivor. I had my books, my teaching,
my poetry. That was exactly how I was. He smiled at the
small blue flower; for the moment, this was the reality. Its
coolness comforted him. It was as if he had returned to a
world before warfare, before secrecy. What a tiny flower
which had somehow survived, like himself. It was like a mirror of himself. Beauty is secrecy, he thought – yet I wonder.
It is too late for the blue flower. The blue flower is a lie.

And he was about to tear it out of the ground. He stretched
his hand forward and touched it. It could not be allowed to
live in such an illusion. He knelt before it in a predatory manner. At that precise moment there was an explosion – a big
red flower blazing above him, about him. The mine must
have been there all the time without his noticing it, mocking
him. The world exploded in rays like one of the wheels of the
carts carrying the old useless gods.

The Dead Man and the Children

THE child gazed at me from the doorway, his eyes innocent as the sky. His head was alive with curls: he looked like a cherub in a picture by an Italian painter. Beside him was a little girl who suddenly stood up, climbed on the piano stool, and began to bang the keys. She looked as demented as a real pianist.

'We'll have to be going to the funeral,' said my wife. I agreed. The child's father, who was our son, put on his black tie while the child stared at him with the same innocent round eyes. His father lifted his son on to his shoulders: the child screamed with delight, pulling at his father's tie.

We drove to the church. The coffin lay at the front. The minister, who was a young man with a beard, said 'There is no death: I am the Way, the Truth, and the Life. In my father's house are many mansions and if it were not so I would have told you.'

The man in the coffin was a relative of ours. In his life he had been generous and courageous: he had died in hospital from cancer bravely borne. Now he was at peace.

The child stood in the sunlight which flickered around him. He touched the little girl wonderingly and then moved away from her, staring at us, his thumb in his mouth. She found a can in a box and began to bang it on the floor. Neither of them could talk much.

The minister intoned words from the Bible. The dead man's wife came in and sat in the front flanked by her daughter and son–in–law who both looked serious. Her relatives were big

156

men from the island, strong, and robust. They sat in a row behind her. 'How handsome they are,' my wife whispered. Big men, solid and strong: they came from the island and ate good food and worked hard and were not sensitive. It seemed to me that they looked like big stones which had stood on a moor since the beginning of time.

The minister was actually quite a small man but extraordinarily intense. He seemed really to believe that there was no death, that death is an alteration and not an end, that we go through a sunny doorway into another more perfect world.

The child and the little girl played with each other in the sunlight. Then they chased a rainbow-coloured ball behind a sofa, their heads close together. The girl was much more active than the boy, more, even, aggressive. The boy sometimes stared in wonderment at the world: how could there be guilt in such a world?

When we came out of the church (my wife, myself and our son) the space in front of and beside the building was congested. It took us a long time to manoeuvre our way out and reach the cemetery even though there was a policeman directing the traffic. We parked the car and walked between the tall steel gates. The streets of the graveyard were straight and clean: in the distance we could see the sea, which glittered and over which a wandering cold breeze moved hesitantly. In front of us were the strong men from the island, stolid and robust, wearing only jackets in spite of the bitter wind. Their faces were as craggy as rocks. Some of the women cried humbly into handkerchiefs. The men got into position around the coffin, each clutching a cord. The dead man's widow couldn't bear coming to the graveside – 'I have done my duty,' she said, 'I cannot bear it.' We shivered in the wind.

My son said, in the hearing of the big men, 'They are supposed to be handsome, these old men. Mother's glasses need examining.' They smiled affectionately like rocks cracking. The minister wasn't wearing a coat either: young and intense he spoke out of the cold wind. 'There is no death, I am the Way and the Truth, I am the gateway to eternal life.'

The two children were sitting beside each other examining a teddy bear, and poking at its shiny button-like eyes. They looked serious and intent in the sunshine of the kitchen. The man in the coffin had been young once too, he too had stared blue-eyed at the world. He had never expected that he would die in a strange hospital in the terrible city: he had wanted home but it was too late. All his life and even during his cancer he had been courageous: perhaps he had been acting a part, but his courage had nevertheless been real. 'I don't worry,' he would say, 'what's the point of worrying. If you worry you die and if you don't worry you die, so what's the point?' He used to sing songs in an affected voice, especially Irish songs and sometimes Italian ones.

The cords lowered the coffin slowly into the hole in the ground. I heard the thud as they were let drop on the wood; it seemed a very final sound. Am I doing this right, the people who were holding the cords would be thinking, I don't want to make a mistake, for the people round the graveside will be watching every move. Then the purple cloth was dropped on top of the coffin and then the wreaths. I could no longer see the coffin at all.

The broad men in front of us turned round and began to talk to us. They were going back to the island the following day: there was the land to be tended to and the cattle, now that spring was approaching. The boat trip would take five hours or so. They didn't seem at all cold in the strong bitter wind which blew in from the blue wrinkled sea.

The eyes of the child were intensely blue. They were like a serene guiltless sky. For ages he would stare at us unwinkingly as if judging us, as if saying, I dare you to stare back at me so unblinkingly. His hands tugged at his father's black tie. Then he stood in the sunlight and seemed eternal.

We walked away from the graveside talking. There was one woman in particular who couldn't remember the names of her relatives. 'Is that Donald or is it James?' she would say. 'I'm so stupid.' A man told of snow in the town from which he had come. 'Six inches,' he said. 'Here it is so mild.' 'How tall you have grown,' said one furred lady to our son. The big men were like moving stones. It didn't look as if any of them would ever die. There was so much to be done on the croft: a new tractor had just been bought and one of the sons used it a lot, playing a radio from it which could be heard all over the village.

The two children touched each other. 'Up,' said the little girl, and my wife lifted her on to the piano stool where she began to bang the keys again while the other child clapped his hands, delighting in the din.

The man had been left in his coffin, which looked like a cradle. Perhaps he had stepped out of it and was elsewhere. Perhaps his soul, white as a gull, had flown into the sun.

The child sat in his high chair banging with his spoon. The little girl gazed at him: he banged and banged as if he were playing a tune. His father raised him up to the ceiling and he shrieked with laughter and excitement. The sun shone on the living-room lighting up the music set, the fireplace, the yellow brassy bin, the statuette of the Virgin, tall and white, with the child in her arms. She was holding Him out to the world: and yet He was the world.

The minister intoned, 'Nothing shall separate us from the love of God.'

We sang, The Lord's my Shepherd: it was not in the hymn book under the number the minister had said, but we all knew the words. They came back to us from our childhood, exact and true and poignant. Wasn't it strange that we knew them, though we didn't know that we did. My table Thou hast furnished in presence of my foes... The child made a paste of its food seriously and obsessively and then chucked some of it on the floor.

Our feet crackled on pebbles as we left the grave: nothing could be seen but the flowers. We asked each other about cars, distances. Some were going to the hotel for a meal, some not. The men from the islands were going to the hotel. They spoke to us secretively in Gaelic: it was like belonging to a separate mysterious world. I couldn't help remembering the poem, The eternal sound of the sea, listen to the eternal sound of the sea. The dead man was sleeping by the sound of the sea. It was better for him to be here than in Glasgow in a stiff shroud, a stranger in a strange city.

The child banged his spoon against the plate. The little girl clapped her hands. They belonged to another world, or did they? They were secretive strangers. On the other hand they were like us and would become like us, but at the moment they looked beautiful and immortal with their cherubic curls. The cradle shone and glittered like a coffin. The child had a pair of yellow shoes, his first ones. Everything was honey-coloured, even the sunlight that lay in bars across the floor.

The big tall men sat down at the table and ate heartily. Tomorrow they would return to their island. They laughed and told jokes from their childhood. The dead man seemed like a pretext for a feast, for laughter, for joy. How odd that death should bring us all together like this.

Bang, bang, went the spoon. The little girl clapped her hands. Maybe in the coffin the dead man clapped his hands too. Maybe he was like a tiny baby in his cradle, blue eyes reflecting the blue sky above him.

A Night with Kant

EACH evening Kant went for a walk. And as he walked he brooded about the Categorical Imperative. It seemed to him that the Categorical Imperative was as fixed as the sun.

One night he saw a beggar beating up his woman, hitting her across the face over and over again. The beggar wore a long coat and his face was unshaven.

'Shall I tell him about the Categorical Imperative?' he asked himself, but decided against it, though the woman was screaming with a loud piercing voice.

'You old fart, I'll kill you,' the beggar shouted. One eye shone madly in his head.

Kant walked on in his neat suit. A watch ticked in his breast pocket. It seemed to him as he looked at the stars that the beggar and the woman were both necessary parts of the universe, as a mainspring was part of a watch.

Another time he saw a thief stealing along with a bagful of stuff he had taken from a shop in which a window was starred and broken.

'No, I'll not tell on him,' he thought. 'I will let him go on his way. Why should I interfere? I am not God.' The thief glared at him with piercing eyes as if saying, 'If you tell anyone what I have done I will kill you.'

Kant wondered what the mind of the thief was like, why he had stolen. He was troubled by the quick bright eyes, the eyes of a man who knew he was doing wrong and enjoying the sensation of it.

How beautiful the stars were, that glittering city which

seemed like a remote reflection of a real city. He imagined the
stars as the souls of the dead, glittering. How really happy he
was to be doing what he was doing. There was no one happier;
he needed no other human being, he needed only his mind,
the universe, that was all.

Yet sometimes he was disturbed by strange thoughts. What
if the world that he was seeing was an unreal spectral world?
What if there was nothing out there that he could trust? What
if there had been no thief at all, no beggar, no screaming
woman? But he put these thoughts away from him as quickly
as they had come. Why should he need a witness? Why couldn't
he depend only on himself?

Another night a policeman stopped him and said, 'Who are
you? Why are you walking about the streets every night?'

'I am a philosopher,' said Kant. 'I am thinking.'

The policeman looked at him suspiciously.

'I thought, sir,' he said, 'that you were following that young
girl.'

'What young girl?' said Kant.

'Never mind,' said the policeman.

Such a self-contained little man this was, such a funny precise man. Perhaps indeed he had been following that girl. You
could never tell with these oldish people.

Kant wondered whether he should mention the Categorical
Imperative to the policeman. He couldn't understand how the
latter's mind worked. In fact it seemed to him that he didn't
understand how anyone's mind worked, except perhaps his
own. The policeman too he considered had a secret violent
eye. He was beginning to wonder whether the world was
more treacherous, phantasmal, than he had originally considered it to be.

Once he heard two women talking. One was saying to the
other, gesturing furiously, 'One should stand up for what one
believes in. Speak straight out, that is what I think.' Later he
heard the same woman saying, 'It doesn't help to be blunt

nowadays. It's better to kowtow and take your hat off to your superiors.'

Kant couldn't understand how people could be so irrational, so contradictory. He wondered if perhaps the world was divided into two groups, the philosophers and the others. Nor could he understand how people were so noticing of the world around them, more noticing than he was.

For instance he heard some men talking about a factory which had just been built. He had passed it every night and yet he hadn't even seen it. Yet these men had studied it in minute detail.

'They shouldn't have a building like that one there,' one man was saying. 'It's ugly, that's what it is. It doesn't fit in.'

And the other man who was bald and fat, said, 'They shouldn't have hired a local firm. Do you know that they take much longer to finish the work? They take advantage, that's what they do.'

Kant gazed vaguely at the factory with its many windows. How had he not noticed it before? And yet factories were useful, they produced commodities. It occurred to him that he knew nothing about the workings of bakeries, butchers' shops, nor did he know what butchers or bakers thought of, or how they conducted their lives. Yet he knew about the Categorical Imperative which they knew nothing of, and conducted their lives in ignorance of it.

What is wrong with me, he asked himself, how do I not have eyes like other people?

And it troubled him that he was so stupid as not to have noticed a factory like that rising from a site where before there had only been emptiness. Again he was stirred by vague guilty feelings. Could it be that these people knew more about the world than he did? Could it be that mice, dogs, cats and rats were more knowledgeable than he was? Could it be that people were secretly laughing at him because he appeared such a fool with his head in the clouds? Or perhaps at the same time as they thought this they also thought that he was a clever man, cleverer than they were themselves. And yet he didn't feel himself to be clever at all. On the contrary he felt himself to be stupid, stupider than the men and women who noticed factories, and were aware of the inner workings of machines.

Once he talked to a man whose job was building houses. 'You put the foundations in first,' the man said to him. 'But sometimes you get a fellow coming from headquarters and he will tell you that the foundations aren't deep enough, so you have to dig deeper. Dampness is one of the things you have to watch for when you are building a house. Condensation you have to look out for on windows. And you should make sure that the house blends in with its surroundings. All these things you have to remember. What do you do yourself?'

'Nothing,' said Kant, 'I am retired.' He was ashamed to tell the man that he was a philosopher, that he sat in a study with books and pen and paper, and that he spent most of his time thinking.

'I hope to be retired myself some day,' said the man, 'but at the moment I can't afford to do that.'

'Why not?' said Kant.

'Well, it's like this,' said the man. 'It's to do with my wife. She says I would be in her way in the house. Women are funny, you understand.'

'Yes,' said Kant.

'You see,' the man continued comfortably, 'you have to treat them carefully, as if you were walking on marshy ground. One minute my wife is saying to me, "You're never at home to help about the house, you never put in shelves, you're too tired", and the next moment she's saying, "I don't want you to retire, you'd be in my way. Under my feet." And that's the fashion of it,' said the man philosophically.

'Take this place we're sitting in,' said the man. 'Now you watch that girl there, the one in the yellow apron. Her name is Gretchen and I know for a fact she comes from a poor family. And yet she will turn up her nose if you don't buy more than one cake. You have to watch the lie of the land, same as when you're building a house. Now yourself now, you'll have experience of these things, I don't need to be telling you them. I would say now you had been a schoolmaster.'

'No,' said Kant. 'I don't think of myself as a schoolmaster.'

'Never mind,' said the man confidently. 'I can tell you were a scholar. I was never a scholar. All I ever read were instruction books.'

'Are they difficult to understand?' said Kant curiously.

'Not if you keep your wits about you,' said the man, who in actual fact wore glasses and in his stooping fashion himself looked like a scholar, and not a builder at all. 'I've seen instructions written in languages that I don't know but that doesn't bother me. I have a picture in my head of what the thing is to be like. Instinctive, you understand. Sometimes I don't need an instruction book at all. I'll tell you something,' he continued expansively. 'Once I was putting in plumbing and this contraption came along and I'd never seen one like it before. But I installed it just the same.'

'Is that right?' said Kant.

'Yes, it's right enough. I have this instinct, you understand. Ever since I was a child. Some people don't have it but I do. Now you take that factory out there. I wouldn't have built it like that, and I would have finished it quicker. I wouldn't have put in so many windows but you can't tell these people anything.'

After the man had left, Kant sat looking around him. Sitting in the café were two young people, the girl gazing into the boy's eyes adoringly. She clasped his hands in hers and began to talk animatedly about some party which they had attended the previous night.

'I saw her wearing the same dress before,' the girl was saying, while at the same time she stroked the boy's hands gently. 'The pink one.'

'Is that right?' said the boy, gazing abstractedly into the girl's eyes.

'Of course, silly,' said the girl. 'Didn't you notice? And another thing, she doesn't have to tell me that she's related to the Schumanns. I know for a fact she isn't.'

Kant stood up and went outside. He looked upward. The stars were numerous like seeds, and remote and beautiful and sparkling. Space and time. They were the conditions of man's existence.

He glanced at his watch. It was seven o'clock at night.

As he was walking along he was stopped by a young woman in a short skirt who said to him, 'I can show you a good time.' Her cheeks were artificially red and her legs were muscular and strong.

'The time is seven o'clock,' said Kant mildly. 'It is neither better nor worse.' The young woman looked at him in amazement and then tottered away arrogantly on her high heels. Kant was stirred by a regretful desire, so vague it was no more than a wandering breeze. And at that moment the Categorical Imperative was very distant indeed.

It was like a ghostly axle in the sky.

Around him were feverish images of colour which seemed to speak of freedom. And he felt very peculiar.

'What am I doing in this place?' he asked himself. 'How did I arrive in this street which I walk so punctually every night? I can't understand it.' And it seemed to him that he could have done something different, been something very different. But the shell that he had constructed round himself protected him, and only late at night did he hear howls as if from the centre of space itself.

Purity, purity, he said to himself. Purity is what I need. Simplicity. But how can one be a saint and live in the world? And he clutched firmly at his watch, that round golden globe on which he depended, in its exactitude. Always ticking like his heart. Except that unlike his heart it was renewable.

Another night he saw a woman walking along the street alone, and her nose was as long as that of a witch such as he had once seen in a story-book when he was a child. Yet what a fool he was. Of course there were no witches, and of course that specific woman was not a witch. On the other hand, as he passed her he felt that at any moment she would burst out cackling and shout disgraceful things after him. Of course she couldn't put a spell on him. Naturally not. Yet he saw her in space dancing with an imaginary illuminated broom which was like the Categorical Imperative.

There is something else, he thought, there is. Behind the stars there is something else, behind the houses there is something else. Deep in the earth, in the remote depths of the universe, there is something else. And it is laughing at me. It is mocking me. It is saying, Who do you think you are? It is saying, Look at that silly man with his watch, he thinks he understands it all. But I know, I know, the thing was saying, I know differently. Deep in the roots and in space itself I AM.

And Kant saw a green snake undulating in the sky, a phantasmal shimmering snake.

And he was suddenly shaken with fear. When he held his hand out one of his fingers was trembling. He gazed at it for a long time but it didn't stop shaking. It was like a magnetic needle that had gone crazy.

Once he saw two small children running away after snatching a handbag from an old woman. They disappeared into the darkness as if into a den. The old woman began to weep, and Kant went up to her, put his hand gently on her arm and said, 'Here's some money.'

But the old woman replied, 'No, indeed, I'll not take it. I have never owed anyone anything in my whole life.'

'What, who?' Kant muttered. 'I don't understand.'

'I've never owed a penny,' said the old woman sniffling yet indomitable. 'I saw them. They were two girls.'

'A girl and a boy,' said Kant.

'No, they were two girls,' said the old woman resolutely. 'They were about sixteen years old.'

'Not more than eleven,' said Kant. 'I'm sure they were not more than eleven.'

'Not at all, sixteen they were,' said the old woman definitely.

Suddenly Kant lost his temper and shouted, 'They were not

more than eleven years old and they were both wearing red jackets.'

'Green,' said the old woman. 'As sure as I'm standing here it was green they were wearing. I still have my faculties, you know.' And she glared furiously at Kant.

'Green,' she said, 'and you must come and tell the police that.'

'No,' said Kant, 'I can't do that.'

What a fool the woman was. Of course the children had been wearing red, even allowing for the darkness. They had certainly not been wearing green. On the other hand she was one of the ones he had heard discussing the factory. In fact, she was the woman whom he remembered as saying that such a stink should not be allowed. He turned away from her in case she would force him to go with her to the police station; he had enough to do with his time. It seemed to him that the ground was trembling under his feet, that the universe was quivering like a morass, that perhaps it didn't exist at all. Why, that old woman might say that it was he who had stolen her money. He looked down at his suit, which was yellow in the light of the lamps. He seemed like a jester, a clown. He took out his watch and consulted it: it gazed back at him, reassuringly golden and round. A tranquil moon.

'A good time,' he heard the voice saying seductively. And the words, 'A good time,' echoed in his head. And at that moment he saw her again. It seemed as if she was always there. She was smiling at him, hitching her skirt to show her thighs.

He walked towards her through the harlequin chequered night. 'Categorical Imperative,' said Kant restlessly in his sleep.

What is he talking about? said the young woman to herself as she examined his jacket. A poor Categorical Imperative he had been indeed. Why, he had fallen asleep like a child in her perfumed room. She stretched herself luxuriously, feeling energy like a strong red pulse in her body. She felt complete inside her envelope of flesh; she was very conscious of her own languorous motions. At that moment she wasn't aware of age or of time. With money, what could one not do? One didn't need to bother thinking about a future: the future would take care of itself. As she watched the sleeping philosopher it angered her that he should have money and she none. Or at least he had more than she had. She had such a beautiful body, such taut pointed breasts, and his body was not powerful or muscular at all. Ahead of her through the window she saw a single star winking in the sky. That might be Venus: she wasn't sure. Her mother had once told her, but she couldn't remember things like that. She took the golden watch from his pocket. She could sell it and this poor idiot would never notice its loss, or if he did he would not complain. She knew his kind, a respectable bourgeois to the very core.

The Maze

IT was early morning when he entered the maze and there were still tiny globes of dew on the grass across which he walked, leaving ghostly footprints. The old man at the gate, who was reading a newspaper, briefly raised his head and then gave him his ticket. He was quite easy and confident when he entered: the white handkerchief at his breast flickered like a miniature flag. It was going to be an adventure, fresh and uncomplicated really. Though he had heard from somewhere that the maze was a difficult one he hadn't really believed it: it might be hard for others but not for him. After all wasn't he quite good at puzzles? It would be like any puzzle, soluble, open to the logical mind.

The maze was in a big green park in which there was also a café, which hadn't as yet opened, and on the edge of it there was a cemetery with big steel gates, and beyond the cemetery a river in which he had seen a man in black waterproofs fishing. The river was as yet grey with only a little sparkle of sun here and there.

At first as he walked along the path he was relaxed and, as it were, lounging: he hadn't brought the power of his mind to bear on the maze. He was quite happy and confident too of the outcome. But soon he saw, below him on the stone, evidence of former passage, for there were empty cigarette packets, spent matches, empty cartons of orangeade, bits of paper. It almost irritated him to see them there as if he wished the maze to be clean and pure like a mathematical problem. It was a cool fresh morning and his shirt shone below his jacket, white and sparkling. He felt nice and new as if he had just been unpacked from a box.

When he arrived at the first dead-end he wasn't at all perturbed. There was plenty of time, he had the whole morning in front of him. So it was with an easy mind that he made his way back to try another path. This was only a temporary setback to be dismissed from his thoughts. Obviously those who had designed the maze wouldn't make it too easy, if it had been a group of people. Of course it might only have been one person. He let his mind play idly round the origin of the maze: it was more likely to have been designed by one person, someone who in the evening of his days had toyed idly with a puzzle of this nature: an engineer perhaps or a setter of crosswords. Nothing about the designer could be deduced from the maze: it was a purely objective puzzle without pathos.

The second path too was a dead-end. And this time he became slightly irritated for from somewhere in the maze he heard laughter. When had the people who were laughing come in? He hadn't noticed them. And then again their laughter was a sign of confidence. One wouldn't laugh if one were unable to solve the puzzle. The clear happy laughter belonged surely to the solvers. For some reason he didn't like them; he imagined them as haughty and imperious, negligent, graceful people who had the secret of the maze imprinted on their brains.

He walked on. As he did so he met two of the inhabitants of the maze for the first time. It was a father and son, at least he assumed that was what they were. They looked weary, and the son was walking a little apart from the father as if he was angry. Before he actually caught sight of them he thought he heard the son say, 'But you said it wouldn't take long.' The father looked guilty and hangdog as if he had failed his son in some way. He winked at the father and son as he passed them as if implying, 'We are all involved in the same puzzle.' But at the same time he didn't feel as if he belonged to the same world as they did. For one thing he was unmarried. For another the father looked unpleasantly flustered and the son discontented. Inside the atmosphere of his own coolness he felt superior to them. There was something inescapably dingy about them, especially about the father. On the other hand they would probably not meet again and he might as well salute them as if they were 'ships of the night'. It seemed to him that the father was grey and tired, like a little weary mouse redolent of failure.

He continued on his way. This too was a dead end. There was nothing to do but retrace his steps. He took his handkerchief out of his pocket, for he was beginning to sweat. He hadn't noticed that the sun was so high in the sky, that he had taken so long already. He wiped his face and put his handkerchief back in his pocket. There was more litter here, a fragment of a doll, a torn pair of stockings. What went on in this maze? Did people use it for sexual performance? The idea disgusted him and yet at the same time it argued a casual mastery which bothered him. That people should come into a maze of all places and carry out their practices there! How obscene, how vile, how disrespectful of the mind that had created it! For the first time he began to feel really irritated with the maze as if it had a life of its own, as if it would allow sordid things to happen. Calm down, he told himself, this is ridiculous, it is not worth this harassment.

He found himself standing at the edge of the maze, and over the hedge he could see the cemetery which bordered the park. The sun was flashing from its stones and in places he could see Bibles of open marble. In others the tombstones were old and covered with lichen. Beyond the cemetery he could see the fisherman still angling in his black shiny waterproofs. The rod flashed back from his shoulder like a snake, but the cord itself was subsumed in bright sunlight.

And then to his chagrin he saw that there was a group of young people outside the maze and quite near him. It was they who had been the source of the laughter. One of them was saying that he had done the maze five times, and that it was a piece of cake, nothing to it. The others agreed with him.

They looked very ordinary young people, not even students, just boys from the town, perhaps six or seven years younger than himself. He couldn't understand how they had found the maze easy when he himself didn't and yet he had a better mind, he was sure of that. He felt not exactly envy of them in their assured freedom but rather anger with himself for being so unaccountably stupid. It sounded to him as if they could enter and leave the maze without even thinking about it. They were eating chips from brown paper, and he saw that the café had opened.

But the café didn't usually open till twelve o'clock, and he had entered the maze at half past nine. He glanced at his watch and saw that it was quarter past twelve. And then he noticed something else, that the veins on his wrists seemed to stand out more, seemed to glare more, than he had remembered them doing. He studied both wrists carefully. No, no question about it, his eyes had not deceived him. So, in fact, the maze was getting at him. He was more worried than he had thought.

He turned back down the path. This time something new had happened. He was beginning to feel the pressure of the maze, that was the only way that he could describe it. It was almost as if the maze were exerting a force over him. He stopped again and considered. In the beginning, when he had entered the maze in his white shirt, which now for some reason looked soiled, he had felt both in control of himself and the maze. It would be he who would decide what direction he would take, it would be he who would remain detached from the maze, much as one would remain detached from a cross-word puzzle while solving it in front of the fire in the evening. But there had been a profound change which he only now recognised. The maze was in fact compelling him to choose, pushing him, making demands on him. It wasn't simply an arrangement of paths and hedges. It was as if the maze had a will of its own.

Now he began to walk more quickly as if feeling that he didn't have much time left. In fact he had an appointment with Diana at three o'clock and he mustn't break it. It would be ridiculous if he arrived late and said, 'I couldn't come because I was powerless to do so. I was a prisoner.' She was sure to think such an explanation odd, not to say astonishing. And in any case if he arrived late she wouldn't be there. Not that deep down he was all that worried, except that his non-appearance would be bad manners. If he was going to give her a pretext for leaving him, then it must be a more considered pretext than that.

He noticed now that his legs were becoming tired and heavy. He supposed that this was quite logical, as the stone would be absorbing some of the energy that he was losing. But what bothered him more than anything was the feeling that it would be a long time before he would get out of the maze, that he was going round in circles. Indeed he recognized some of the empty cigarette packets that he was passing. They were mostly Players and he was sure that he had seen them before. In fact he bent down and marked some of them with a pen to make sure of later identification. This was the sort of thing that he had read of in books, people going round and round deserts in circles. And yet he thought that he was taking a different path each time. He wiped his face again and felt that he was losing control of himself. He must be if he was going round and round in helpless circles all the time. Maybe if he had a thread or something like that he would be able to strike out on fresh paths. But he didn't have a thread and some remnant of pride determined that he would not use it, rather like his resolve not to use a dictionary except as a last resort when he was doing a crossword puzzle. He must keep calm. After all, the café and the cemetery were quite visible. It wasn't as if he was in a prison and couldn't shout for help if the worst came to the worst. It wasn't as if he was stranded on a desert island. And yet he knew that he wouldn't shout for help: he would rather die.

He didn't see the father and son again but he saw other people. Once he passed a big heavy man with large black-rimmed spectacles who had a brief-case in his hand, which he thought rather odd. The man, who seemed to be in a hurry, seemed to know exactly where he was going. When they passed each other the man didn't even glance at him, and didn't smile. Perhaps he looked contemptible to him. It was exactly as if the man was going to his office and the path of the maze was an ordinary high road.

Then again he saw a tall ghostly-looking man passing, and he turned and stared after him. The man was quite tall, not at all squat like the previous one. He looked scholarly, abstracted and grave. He seemed to drift along, inside an atmosphere of his own, and he himself knew as if by instinct that the first man would have no difficulty in solving the riddle of the maze but that the second would. He didn't know how he knew this, but he was convinced just the same. The maze he now realized was infested with people, men, women and children, young people, old people, middle-aged people. Confident people and ghostly people. It was like a warren and he felt his bones shiver as the thought came to him. How easy it had been to think at the beginning that there was only himself: and now there were so many other people. People who looked straight ahead of them and others who looked down at the ground.

One in particular, with the same brisk air as the black-spectacled man, he had an irresistible desire to follow. The man was grey-haired and soldierly. He, like the first one, didn't look at him or even nod to him as he passed, and he knew that this was another one who would succeed and that he should follow him. But at the same time it came to him that this would be a failure of pride in himself, that he didn't want to be like a dog following its master as if he were on a string. The analogy disgusted him. He must not lose control of his will, he must not surrender it to someone else. That would be nauseating and revolting.

He noticed that he was no longer sweating and this bothered him too. He should be sweating, he should be more frightened. Then to his amazement he saw that the sun had sunk quite far in the direction of the west. He came to a dead halt almost in shock. Why was time passing so rapidly? It must be four o'clock at least and when he glanced at his watch he saw that it was actually half past four. And therefore he had missed Diana. What a ludicrous thing. This maze, inert and yet malevolent, was preventing him from doing what he ought to have done and forcing him to do other things instead. Probably he would never see Diana again. And then the thought came to him, threatening in its bareness, what if he had chosen to walk into this maze in order to avoid her? No, that was idiotic. Such an idea had never come into his head. Not for one moment.

He looked down at his shoes and saw that they were white with dust. His trousers were stained. He felt smelly and dirty. And what was even more odd when he happened to see the backs of his hands he noticed that the hair on them was grey. That surely couldn't be. But it was true, the backs of his hands had grey hair on them. Again he stood stock-still trying to take account of what had happened. But then he found that he couldn't even stand still. It was as if the maze had accelerated. It was as if it could no longer permit him to think objectively and apart from himself. Whenever a thought came into his head it was immediately followed by another thought which devoured it. He had the most extraordinary vision which hit him with stunning force. It was as if the pathways in his brain duplicated the pathways of the maze. It was as if he was walking through his own brain. He couldn't get out of the maze any more than he could get out of his own head. He couldn't quite focus on what he sensed, but he knew that what he sensed or thought was the truth. Even as he looked he could see young people outside the café. They seemed amazingly young, much younger than he had expected. They were not the same ones as the early laughers, they were different altogether, they were young children. Even their clothes were different. Some of them were sitting eating ice-cream at a table which stood outside the café and had an awning over it. He couldn't remember that awning at all. Nor even the table. The fisherman had disappeared from the stream. The cemetery seemed to have spawned more tombstones.

His mind felt slow and dull and he didn't know where to go

next. It came to him that he should sit down where he was and make no more effort. It was ludicrous that he should be so stupid as not to get out of the maze which others had negotiated so easily. So he couldn't be as intelligent as he thought he was. But it was surely the maze that was to blame, not himself. It quite simply set unfair problems, and those who had solved them had done so by instinct like animals. He remembered someone who had been cool and young and audacious and who had had a white handkerchief in his pocket like a flag. But the memory was vaguer than he had expected, and when he found the handkerchief it was only a small crumpled ball which was now in his trouser pocket. He turned and looked at the flag which marked the centre of the maze. It seemed that he would never reach it.

He felt so sorry for himself that he began to cry a little and he couldn't stop. Water drooled from his eyes, and he wiped it away with his dirty handkerchief. There didn't seem to be so many people in the maze now. It was a stony wilderness. If there was one he could recognize as successful he would follow him like a dog. He would have no arrogance now. His brow puckered. There was someone he remembered as existing outside the maze, someone important, someone gracious, elegant, a magnet which he had somehow lost. She was... but he couldn't remember who she was. And in any case had she been outside the maze? Had she not always been inside it, perhaps as lost as he was himself?

Slowly and stubbornly he plodded on, no longer imagining that he would leave the maze, walking for the sake of walking. The twilight was now falling, and the café was shut. He could hear no sounds around him, no infestation of the maze, and yet strangely enough he sensed that there were beings there. If he could no longer escape from the maze then he might at least reach the centre and see what was there. Perhaps some compensating emblem, some sign, some pointer to the enigma. Perhaps even the designer of the maze sitting there in a stony chair. He set his teeth, he must not give in. He must not allow the thought to control him that he had no power over the maze, that in fact the power was all the other way. That would be the worst of all, not only for him but for everybody else.

And then quite ironically, as if the seeing of it depended on his thought, there was the centre, barer than he had expected, no emblem, no sign, no designer.

. All that was there was a space, and a clock and a flag. The clock pointed to eleven. The sun was setting, red and near in the sky. It was a big ball that he might even clutch. The twilight was deepening. For a moment there, it was as if in the centre of the maze he had seen a tomb, but that couldn't be true. That must have come from his brooding on the cemetery. On the other hand it might be a cradle. And yet it wasn't that either. There was nothing there at all, nothing but the space on which the paths converged.

He looked at the space for a long time, as if willing something to fill it. And then very slowly from the three other paths he saw three men coming. They seemed superficially to be different, but he knew that they were all the same. That is to say, there hovered about the faces of each of them a common idea, a common resemblance, though one was dressed in a grey suit, one in a gown, and one in jacket and flannels. They all stood there quite passively and waited for him to join them. They were all old. One of them to his astonishment held a child by the hand. He stood there with them. Slowly the sun disappeared over the horizon and darkness fell and he felt the pressure of the maze relaxing, as if in a dream of happiness he understood that the roads were infinite, always fresh, always new, and that the ones who stood beside him were deeper than friends, they were bone of his bone, they were flesh of his disappearing flesh.